D0906183

DUSTY BARNETT

Other Books Available by James Clay:

Matheson's Legacy
Boyd Matheson

DUSTY BARNETT

•

James Clay

AVALON BOOKS
NEW YORK

Library of Congress Cataloging-in-Publication Data

Clay, James.
   Dusty Barnett / James Clay.
      p. cm.
   ISBN 978-0-8034-7790-2
   1.   Sheriffs—Fiction.   2.   Theatrical companies—Fiction.
3.   Arizona—Fiction.   I.   Title.
   PS3603.L387D87 2010
   813'.6—dc22
                                                    2010016288

PRINTED IN THE UNITED STATES OF AMERICA
ON ACID-FREE PAPER
BY HADDON CRAFTSMEN, BLOOMSBURG, PENNSYLVANIA

For Kristin and Jeremiah: two straight shooters
who ride tall in the Badlands.

Chapter One

Sheriff Dusty Barnett nodded to several familiar faces as he approached the church, but his attention was focused on a stranger. The young man had ridden into town earlier with anger and determination bursting in his eyes. Those eyes hadn't changed much, and the kid met the lawman's gaze with a look that spelled challenge.

Dusty figured he would let the kid stew a bit; it might help some. The lawman then laughed inwardly at his own method. In his twenty plus years of wearing a star, he had found that giving a hothead time to cool off rarely worked. Still . . .

The sheriff shifted his focus to the man in a black frock coat who now approached him. "Evening, Reverend. Too bad you can't get this many folks into the church on Sunday morning. Almost the whole town is here."

"Not quite." Reverend Paul Colten looked about sheepishly. "Several members of my flock have informed me that I've turned God's house over to the devil

1

himself. They're off somewhere plotting how to run me out of town."

Barnett gave the pastor a lopsided smile. "I have wondered what made you decide to let a theatrical troupe put on a play in the church."

"Brett Connors," the clergyman answered. "Brett has done a lot for this town. He believes that bringing a theater company to Dawson will help to make the town more, oh, *civilized*, I guess is the word. I agree."

Barnett nodded. "I guess the church is about the only place in town to do a play."

This time it was the reverend who gave a lopsided smile. "They could have used one of the bars, but enough of this town's business is already conducted in bars. I'd better get inside. Brett wants me to say a few words before curtain time."

Barnett gave the parson a questioning stare. The clergyman replied with a mischievous grin. " 'Curtain time'—that's theater talk. I picked it up while attending school in the east." He hurried off.

Dusty Barnett now returned his full attention to the sullen-looking stranger. The young man no longer wore the gun that had pressed against his right hip when the sheriff spotted him entering the Fast Horse Saloon. The stranger knew that guns would not be permitted inside a church. Even Sheriff Barnett had left his .44 in the office.

The man had red hair, red freckles, bloodshot eyes, and lips pressed together. Barnett knew the expression well. The young man had entered the saloon looking for courage, and he had found it.

The lawman casually approached the stranger. "Good evening."

The young man nodded.

The sheriff extended his hand. "The name is Dusty Barnett."

"Abel." He offered his hand reluctantly.

"Well, Abel, I hope you enjoy—"

"I plan to have a real good time, Sheriff!" He looked contemptuously at the star on Barnett's vest. "Yeah, you just leave me alone, and I'll enjoy myself fine!"

Abel's hands folded into fists. He looked toward the sky, and whatever he saw there only made him more angry. "Just leave me alone," he repeated, and then he joined the crowd that was now ambling into the church. By the time Barnett got inside, Abel was sitting at the end of the third pew from the front, right beside the center aisle.

The lawman leaned against a back wall beside the wide double door that was the church's only entrance and exit. His eyes scanned the crowd, which consisted mostly of townspeople he had known for years. His deputy, Caleb Hodge, gave him a quick salute from one of the back pews. Caleb was sitting with Phoebe Martin, a young lady he had been courting for several months. Phoebe turned and smiled at Barnett, who nodded in a courteous manner.

All of the pews were packed tightly. Brett Connors

approached the sheriff and stood beside him. "Maybe this wasn't such a good idea."

"What do you mean?"

Connors was a sandy-haired man in his late twenties. Raised in the east, he had adjusted quickly to the western way of life after moving to Dawson, Arizona, to take over the operation of the stagecoach line following his uncle's death. "Don't get me wrong, I think bringing culture to this town is a good idea. But these theater folks who arrived today—well, they're, uh, different."

"Do you—" Barnett stopped speaking as Reverend Colten stepped onto the raised platform that fronted the choir loft at the front of the church.

"Good evening. Almost all of you know me. On formal occasions some folks call me Reverend Paul Colten, but I prefer Reverend Colt. It's nice and short. People tell me that I should try to make my sermons the same way."

Good-natured laughter filled the church. Dusty Barnett knew that Reverend Colt had a gift for putting people at ease. He hoped that ability included those folks who were angry about the church being used for a theater.

The pastor continued to speak. "This week the Dawson Community Church will house our town's very first play. Tickets will be twenty-five cents for adults and ten cents for anyone under the age of sixteen. No charge for babies being carried in their mother's arms. These low prices are possible because Brett Connors paid the expenses of the theatrical company to come here. Back east they would call Brett a benefactor. Let's give our benefactor some applause!"

"I didn't want him to say that—honest," Brett whispered to the sheriff as he acknowledged the clapping.

Reverend Colt continued as soon as the applause subsided. "Many of you have never had the opportunity to see a play before. Therefore, the Lamont Theatrical Company has agreed to provide this free preview of their melodrama, *The Phantom Killer,* which will be presented two nights from now. I present the head of the Lamont Theatrical Company, Mr. Victor Lamont."

There was an uneasy moment as a man hastily arose from the first pew and stepped onto the platform. As Reverend Colt stepped off, he made a quick clapping motion with his hands. The audience began to applaud.

"Thank you, good citizens of Dawson." Victor Lamont was a tall, wide-shouldered man, stocky but not fat. "On each side of me you can see that we have erected barriers, using the kind of screens that you might find in any home. In between these screens is a very special area that shall serve as a stage for our melodrama."

With a dramatic flourish Lamont took two steps to his left and paused in front of one of the barriers, holding up one arm in the direction of the "stage." "This is the large guest room on the second floor of Winslow Castle in rural England. Connie Smith has just arrived from Ohio to visit her cousin, who married a wealthy Englishman. . . ."

As Victor spoke, a young woman stepped from behind the screen on the left side of the stage. She pretended to open a door and then quickly moved to a chair, which was the only actual piece of furniture on the stage. The actress pretended to comb her hair as she looked into a mirror that wasn't there. Another, slightly older woman followed her and pantomimed knocking on the door. Both women were beautiful, and there were murmurs of appreciation from some of the men in the audience. But the whispering soon died down. The murmurers, like everyone else, were caught up in the spectacle before them.

Barnett was both confused and fascinated. This should look silly—there was no castle. People were pretending to open doors that didn't exist. And yet, it seemed sort of real. The sheriff folded his arms and continued to watch.

"Come in." The woman pretending to comb her hair had the first line.

Victor Lamont returned to the front pew.

The other actress stepped through the make-believe door and pretended to close it. "My dear Connie, before you retire for the night, there is something I must warn you about."

Connie bolted from her chair and approached her cousin. "Elizabeth, there is a worried countenance on your face. What has put it there?"

Elizabeth's eyes grew wide as she turned to face the audience. "There are nights when, from my bedroom window, I spot a most horrible creature. An apparition dressed in black, with a face the color of fire. He stares at me with a wicked, evil scowl. On some nights I have even spotted him while strolling through the gardens. He laughs mockingly, then covers his horrible face with a cape and seems to vanish into the darkness of the night."

The audience in the small church sat totally still. Barnett noticed that even the small boys were no longer fidgeting.

"Dear Elizabeth!" Connie's exclamation caused several people to jump in their seats. "Have you told Lord Stanley about this?"

"Yes, my dear husband has summoned Dr. Philip Grayson to stay with us for a while."

"Oh, yes, the doctor I met at dinner this evening," Connie replied. "Do you think he can cure you of these terrible hallucinations?"

Elizabeth paused dramatically, her eyes seeming to scan the audience. "I am not hallucinating!"

"My precious cousin, you must—"

Elizabeth whirled to face the younger woman. "Eight months ago an entire family perished when a fire ravaged Brinthrope Hall. The fire was set deliberately. That happened less than one day's ride from here."

"Oh, unspeakable horror!" Connie clasped a hand over her forehead and took a step backward. "And you believe this strange apparition you see could be the killer?"

"Yes, dear cousin, but we are both weary. We shall

speak more of these matters in the morning." Elizabeth hugged her cousin, then once again stepped through a door that didn't exist and vanished behind the left partition.

Connie placed a hand over her mouth in an exaggerated yawn. "My trip has left me very tired." She quickly returned to the chair as she spoke. "But before turning in, I should finish combing my . . ." Connie's words became slurred as she fell asleep in her chair.

From behind the left partition, a figure clothed entirely in black, including a flat-brimmed hat, emerged. A number of children in the audience began to scream. The figure advanced toward the fictional door, while holding a cape in front of its face. The screaming grew louder as the frightening apparition stepped into the guest room and moved stealthily toward the sleeping Connie. Several people in the audience turned their heads toward the sheriff, who could only shrug his shoulders in response.

Connie awoke, jumped from her chair, and gave a scream that overwhelmed the noise from the audience and left the crowd in a startled silence. The young woman collapsed to the floor in a faint. Loud footsteps could be heard from behind the left partition.

The figure in black pretended to open a window. Before stepping out, he lowered his cape to reveal a bright red face and set off another chorus of screams from the audience. He then pantomimed a climb through the window and vanished behind the right partition.

A young man appeared from behind the opposite partition, ran to the door that didn't exist, and entered the room. "Miss Smith!" He knelt over Connie and gently slapped her on the face. The young woman revived. "Dr. Grayson . . ."

"Allow me to help you to your feet." The doctor placed his arms around Connie as she stood up.

"This ain't right! You git away from her!" The freckle-faced young man Barnett had spoken to outside the church bolted from his seat and ran toward the actors.

Barnett had been completely caught up in the spectacle before him and was startled by the actions of the man he had earlier identified as a troublemaker. "Is this part of the play?" he whispered to Brett Connors.

"I don't think so."

The young man took a short hop onto the platform and pushed Dr. Grayson to the floor. "You stay away from her—I mean it!" He turned to the actress. "Hilda, you're coming back to Tucson with me!"

Hilda, the actress who had been playing Connie Smith, looked scornfully at the man who had invaded the stage. "What kind of woman do you take me for, Abel Jacklin? Let me be!"

Abel reached out a hand toward the actress. "Now, you jus' listen. . . ."

Dusty Barnett trotted down the aisle, then stepped quietly but quickly onto the platform. "Take it easy cowboy. You—"

"Stay outta this!" Abel turned and made a wild swing with his right arm in the sheriff's direction. The crowd began to shout, scream, and laugh.

Dusty Barnett delivered a hard jab to Abel's midriff and pushed the young man off the platform. As Abel hit the floor, Barnett held up two hands in a "stop" gesture, trying to calm the situation.

Abel would have none of that. As he returned to his feet, his face was twisted with humiliation and the need for revenge. "I told you to stay outta this. Now I'm gonna *make* you stay out."

The fire in the young man's eyes was intense and needed to be doused fast. Abel hadn't completely regained his balance when Barnett hopped off the platform and slammed a fist into the kid's right cheek. Once again Abel plunged to the floor, and this time Barnett was confident that he wouldn't come up fighting.

"Abel!" Hilda hastily lifted her skirts over her ankles, stepped off the platform, then kneeled over the fallen young man and began to help him to his feet.

Barnett noted that the scene taking place beside him was a bit like the one that was being performed when the play was abruptly stopped.

"Why did you have to go do such a fool thing?" Hilda's face contorted as tears covered her cheeks. She wasn't acting.

"I couldn't watch that guy put his arm around ya." Abel's words were slurred as he struggled to stay on his feet. Abel wasn't acting either. "I love ya, Hilda. I want ya to—"

"Well, why didn't you tell me that back in Tucson?" Hilda was now crying uncontrollably.

"There are some things a man shouldn't hafta—" Abel suddenly stopped speaking and gave the young woman a firm kiss on the lips. When their lips parted, Hilda began to laugh in a giddy manner. She turned her head hastily toward the troupe's leader. "Sorry, Mr. Lamont . . ."

Arms entwined, Hilda and Abel ran down the center aisle of the church together and out the door. The audience, a bit dazed by all that they had witnessed, began to cheer.

Victor Lamont was now standing beside Barnett. A chagrined look creased his face as he watched the couple exit. "I pity that poor young woman."

Barnett could barely hear Lamont for all of the raucous shouts and laughter. "Why's that?"

"She will spend the rest of her life on some ranch, looking after cows and a horde of brats. And all the time she will be daydreaming about the time when she was an actress, when life was special and she could take a bow." Lamont shook his head sadly and then continued. "Shakespeare was right—'What fools these mortals be!' "

The cheers were subsiding, and people were starting to shout out questions about when the entire play would be performed. Barnett had a feeling that he would have to deal with a lot more "foolish mortals" before this theatrical company left town.

But he didn't know how deadly the foolishness would become.

Chapter Two

B rett Connors looked sheepish as he sat in front of the sheriff's desk. "I just came from a meeting with Victor Lamont. The theatrical company is going to stay in town for a few more days. Lamont says they will be able to do the play on Saturday night."

Dusty Barnett cupped his hands behind his head, looked across the desk, and gave Connors a concerned smile. "That means you'll have to pay out more money to keep those folks at the hotel."

The manager of the stage depot waved a hand as if dismissing the problem. "You know, I've had an eye on that hotel, thinking about buying it."

"Stagecoach business not so good?"

"Business is great—now. But everyone is talking about how the railroad may come through Dawson."

"Only maybe," Barnett said casually. "There are other places being considered."

"A businessman has to think ahead." Connors pointed a thumb at himself. "If the railroad does come through, stagecoach business will fall off. But there will be plenty of need for a good hotel."

The sheriff's mind stayed in the present. "Saturday night isn't far away. Where is that theatrical troupe going to find an actress to replace the one who ran off?"

Brett Connors shrugged as a cry of "Sheriff!" came from outside. Nine-year-old Jimmy Ellis fell as he ran into the office. "Sheriff Barnett, you gotta go quick! Right outside of town—Pa is in trouble."

Barnett jumped up and lifted the boy onto his feet. "Calm down, Jimmy. Tell me what happened."

"Pa and me was ridin' into town from the farm when we heard shots."

"Yes, go on."

"Three fellers were tryin' to hold up the stage."

Dusty could see Brett Connors' body tense up. "Were they chasing the stagecoach?" the sheriff asked.

"Yeah, but the stage was goin' fast. Mighta outrun 'em, but a wheel busted or somethin', and the stage had to stop. The guy ridin' shotgun was good. He forced the robbers up a hill. Two of them are behind a big boulder. The other one is behind another boulder."

"Good old Hawk Pickford, best shotgun rider in the Arizona Territory!" Brett Connors banged a fist into his right palm.

"Not right now," Jimmy responded. "One of them outlaws got lucky and hit the shotgun rider."

"How badly is he hurt?" Connors shouted.

"Don't know. The driver's a good shot too. But he

can't handle three outlaws by himself. Bet them hard cases got plenty of ammo. Pa rode in to help the driver hold them off. Sent me to get help."

"Are there any passengers?" Barnett grabbed a Winchester from a rack behind his desk. Connors was on his feet.

"I couldn't see any. Maybe they were hidin' in the coach."

"How far away are they, Jimmy?" the sheriff asked.

"Where those four big mesquite trees stand together."

"My horse is tied up right outside the depot." Brett Connors ran his words together. "Meet me there." He bolted from the office. Barnett and the boy followed him.

On the boardwalk outside the office, the sheriff hastily looked about. "Jimmy, I need you to find my deputy."

"Caleb Hodge?"

"Yes, he's on a round, probably near the bank. Tell him what happened. He'll need to bring Dr. Jamieson with him. Now run, boy!"

Jimmy did as he was told. The sheriff mounted the Appaloosa that he had tethered outside the office and rode to the depot where Brett Connors was mounting his bay.

The two men spurred their steeds into a fast gallop. For a man still new to the west, Connors rode well. But Barnett noted that the businessman did have some problems keeping control of his horse.

The sheriff pulled ahead of his companion and signaled him to follow as he took a path that veered to the left of the road. The path ran to the back of the hill where the gunmen were trying to move in on the stage.

Both riders slowed as they heard gunshots. Barnett nodded at the hill in front of them. "We'll dismount and walk the horses up."

They actually ran as they guided the horses up the hill, then used rocks to tether the animals when they were near the top but still out of sight. Both men pulled rifles from the scabbards of their saddles and proceeded cautiously to the pinnacle of the mound, where they had a view of the fighting below.

The scene was exactly as Jimmy had described it. Two outlaws were hunkered down behind a large boulder, about twenty yards below where Barnett and Connors were standing. About fifteen feet from the large rock was a smaller boulder, which protected the third gunman.

Jimmy had also been right about the stagecoach. The right front wheel was indeed busted. Hawk Pickford was lying under the coach, firing at the robbers, but he was obviously wounded and seemed close to passing out. Beside him was the stagecoach driver, armed with a Henry identical to Hawk's. A team of frightened horses were dancing about in their harnesses, causing the coach to lurch back and forth.

Tom Ellis was standing behind the back end of the stage. All three men were firing cautiously; their ammo was running out. From inside the coach, a man's head appeared at the window, then immediately ducked down.

There was no cover at all at the top of the hill where Barnett and Connors crouched low, still unseen by the outlaws. The sheriff lay on the ground and motioned for Brett to do the same. "We should be able to—"

As Connors dropped to the ground, Barnett could see that his face was contorted in a look of fear and hatred. The businessman's lips trembled before he spoke. "That's the Rollins gang—I read the wanted circulars. They've robbed and killed and—"

"I read those circulars too," Barnett said hastily. "I'm not sure—"

Brett Connors fired his Winchester. One of the two outlaws behind the large boulder slammed against the rock. His body began to slump downward as Connors levered the rifle. The second outlaw turned with a stunned expression on his face. He raised his right hand, which held a six-shooter; maybe he was going to throw it down and surrender, or maybe he was going to fire. The question would never be answered. Connors' second shot lifted the outlaw's body into a grotesque hop, then tossed him to the ground.

The robber behind the smaller boulder holstered his gun and scrambled toward his horse. "Don't shoot!" Barnett ordered Brett Connors. "I think we can take him alive."

Both men jumped to their feet as Connors shouted, "I'll go after the—"

"You belong here with the stagecoach and your men. First, check those two jaspers down there and make sure they're dead." Barnett knew his advice was a formality. Both men were gone or soon would be.

The sheriff ran to his Appaloosa, mounted, and rode upward to where he could once again view the action. Connors was doing as he had been told. The third crook was spurring his horse into a fast, downward gallop—a good way to ruin a fine animal. Barnett moved cautiously down the hill.

Brett Connors suddenly looked at the lawman with an angry, impatient stare. Barnett understood. One of Brett's best men had just been shot. Connors wanted justice. But maiming the Appaloosa would accomplish nothing.

When he reached flat ground, Barnett spurred his horse into a brisk gallop. They moved fast enough to advance on their prey. The outlaw's chestnut had already been ridden hard in the robbery attempt and was running with little stamina left. The robber fired two shots at the lawman; neither came close to the target. The outlaw holstered his gun and spurred his horse mercilessly. Barnett was dealing with a man in panic.

The chase led to a mountain where the robber obviously hoped to get lost among the caves and caverns. He pushed his chestnut hard as they galloped up a steep slope to a trail that wound up the mountain. The sheriff had just started up the slope as the chestnut gave a terrified neigh and collapsed to the ground. The horse's eyes flared wide, and its legs kicked the air as it skidded downward. Barnett worked to keep his Appaloosa under control and couldn't spot the outlaw as dust clouds swirled around the fallen animal.

The chestnut's skid ended, and the animal returned to its feet. There was an eerie silence. Barnett quickly dismounted, suppressed a cough, then drew his Colt .44 and tethered the roan. He stood alert, observing the dust as it returned to the ground, then cautiously approached the area of the fall. From the corner of his eye he could see that the chestnut, while shaken and exhausted, did not appear seriously injured.

The same could not be said for the horse's rider. At first glance Barnett knew that the man's neck was broken.

Chapter Three

Victor Lamont sat in the first pew of the church watching as Charles Stafford and Bert Lassiter rehearsed a scene from *The Phantom Killer.* For Bert, who had done this play countless times before, it was a matter of getting used to the unusual stage. Stafford, who portrayed the handsome, heroic Dr. Grayson, was having some trouble remembering his lines.

Lamont looked away from the two men as he laughed softly. He couldn't remember why the previous Dr. Grayson had abandoned the troupe in Denver; some problem with the law, in all likelihood. He did remember that Charles Stafford—a phony name probably, just like Victor Lamont—had been very happy to join the company and even happier to leave Denver. Did Stafford's problems involve the law, a woman, gambling debts, or . . . ?

Victor Lamont's laugh turned into a sigh. Actors were such an irresponsible lot. Why didn't he give all this up and—

The doors of the church opened, and his question was answered before he finished asking it. Jessica Lamont walked quickly down the aisle to the front; his beautiful wife loved acting and belonged on the stage. For an uncomfortable moment he wondered if Jessica could ever be content with a life away from audiences and make-believe.

"She's perfect," Jessica declared in a stage whisper.

"What's this girl's name again?" As he spoke, Victor stood up and made a gesture for the two actors to stop rehearsing.

"Phoebe Martin. She works at a restaurant owned by her family."

"That must be Martin's Restaurant!" Pride laced Bert Lassiter's voice as if he had just made a profound observation.

"Correct, Bert." Jessica nodded politely at the actor, then continued. "I spotted her during yesterday's performance. She is the prettiest girl in this town and a lot of other towns for that matter. She'll look great in the costumes."

"You're talking about that incredible blond! I spotted her too," Charles Stafford blurted out. "Boy, is she ever—"

"That's enough!" Victor glared at Stafford, then turned back to his wife. "Do you think she can act?"

"Phoebe Martin is intelligent. She can have her lines memorized by Saturday." A mischievous sparkle radiated from Jessica's eyes. "I pretended to stop in the restaurant to get some information about the town and began to talk to Phoebe about the life of an actress. You should have seen the glow on her face! Oh, yes, she will want to do it, and I believe she will make a wonderful Connie Smith."

Victor again marveled at the very special woman he had married. Jessica was a beautiful woman who had absolutely no jealousy of another woman's beauty. Her only concern was Saturday's performance.

Bert's voice interrupted his musings. "I say let's not take any chances. Wire Mamie Thompson in Denver. She knows the part."

"Out of the question," Victor snapped. "She couldn't get here by Saturday. We've got to pull out Sunday in order to make it to Tombstone. We're booked in a real theater there for three nights and a matinee. Besides, we can't ask Mr. Connors to keep us at the hotel much longer. We need to make what money we can here and get out."

"Brett has been a most generous benefactor."

There was a coyness in Jessica's voice that bothered her husband. His wife seemed to be on a first-name basis with almost every man she met.

Charles Stafford looked a bit confused by the situation. "Do you think this Phoebe gal will come to Tombstone with us?"

Jessica spoke slowly. "I don't know. Perhaps Mamie can join us in Tombstone."

"Right now we must find our Connie Smith for

Dawson," Victor proclaimed in a grand manner to his wife. "Shall we employ the same charade that we used last year in that small town in California?"

"Yes," Jessica replied joyfully. "We are on our way to wire an actress in Denver. We happen to stop by the restaurant, and—"

Victor Lamont thrust out his right arm. "I begin to talk with the young lady and realize that she has all the artistic instincts of a great actress!"

Jessica Lamont giggled with excitement and antici-pation. Victor knew that there was not a touch of mean-ness in her laughter. She was looking forward to the excursion into make-believe.

Victor Lamont took his wife by the arm, and they headed for their next "performance."

Barnett, Caleb Hodge, and Brett Connors sat around a table at the Golden Nugget Saloon. A fourth man sat at the table with them, nervously scribbling in a tablet. At that time in the early afternoon, they were the only customers except for a handful of barflies who were talking to the bartender in a low voice and, apparently, laughing over some private joke.

"Three men dead." Connors stared ruefully into his drink. "And I killed two of them myself. One man I shot in the back."

"First time you were in a gunfight, Brett?" Barnett asked.

Connors nodded. "I took another look at those

circulars before coming over here. I was wrong. That bunch wasn't the Rollins gang. Just three common saddle tramps . . ."

The scribbler, who had been paying no attention to the conversation around him, lifted the tablet and began to read his own words out loud. "A bullet blazed into the stagecoach, knocking the derby off my head. I was in a land of savage barbarians and could remain a man of peace no longer. I grabbed the rifle the driver had tossed down to me and fired—"

"Uh, Mr. Stevens." Caleb Hodge nodded at a hat perched on the table. "Your derby looks fine, and the driver said nothing about—"

Bradley Stevens was clearly irritated by the interruption. "A good reporter must occasionally embellish the facts in order to convey a deeper, more profound truth to his readers."

"Oh." Hodge ran a hand through his brown hair. The hair was thick, not surprising for a man just a year past twenty. The hair topped a small forehead and a sharp nose that well fit his angular body.

"Tell me, Mr. Stevens"—Barnett tried to keep any note of irritation out of his voice—"just why did this newspaper of yours, the . . ."

"*Tribune,* the *Philadelphia Tribune,*" Bradley said hastily.

"Why did the paper send you here?"

Bradley Stevens had a boyish face that radiated a boyish enthusiasm. Like Caleb Hodge he had brown hair, but the hair was thinning, giving a touch of maturity to the reporter's appearance. "Why, our paper received a notice from Mr. Victor Lamont that his theatrical company would be doing a play in a hick town where the local rubes had no idea of what a theater was!"

Brett Connors groaned out loud. "Vic mentioned something about that to me. Sorry . . ."

Dusty Barnett felt genuinely sorry for Connors. "Did you meet Lamont during that trip to Denver a couple months back?"

Connors smiled in a sheepish manner. "Yeah, I've always liked the theater, and I took in a few plays while I was there, including *The Phantom Killer.* After the play, I talked to Lamont and found out that he had a touring company." Brett shrugged.

"Well, it is a magnificent thing you are doing, Mr. Connors," Stevens proclaimed. "Bringing the cleansing uplift of the theater to a people who probably only bathe twice a year." The reporter suddenly closed his mouth, raised his eyebrows, and looked apologetic. Still, he promised himself to use the line in an article; the theater crowd in Philadelphia would love it.

"Thank you for the encouraging words, Mr. Stevens." Connors stood up. "I've got a stagecoach to fix. See you gentlemen later."

As Brett left the saloon, the laughter from the bar became louder. "At the rate they're going, those jaspers will pass out before sundown," Barnett said to his companions.

One of the barflies, Earl Beasely, walked none too steadily toward Caleb Hodge. "Hey, Deputy, I hear that little girlie of yours is going to strut her stuff in front of the whole town." Drunken guffaws came from the bar.

Both lawmen eyed the lout with intense anger. Hodge spoke first. "What are you talking about?"

"Ain't you heard? Miss Phoebe Martin has joined that bunch of acting people."

"That's a lie!" Hodge shot back.

"Don't you call me a liar! Why, next that little girlie will be in some music hall wearin' one of them frilly costumes and—"

Caleb Hodge shot from his chair and slammed a fist into Earl's face. Beasely hit the floor. His companions at the bar began to laugh, then stopped when they saw that Dusty Barnett was on his feet and in no mood for nonsense.

Hodge was seething with anger. The sheriff spoke quietly to his deputy. "Get back to the office. We've got work to do."

"There's somebody I've got to talk to first."

Barnett's voice took on a bit more force. "Get back to the office."

The deputy turned and quickly departed the Golden Nugget. From the floor, Beasely slurred, "That lawdog's got no right to—"

"Shut up." Barnett looked with disdain at Earl Beasely and his companions. "Maybe the law gives you the right to bray like a donkey, but I'm not going to waste much of my time enforcing it. I want all of you jaspers out of town by sunup tomorrow."

One of the men leaning against the bar shouted, "You can't—"

"Yes, I can."

As Barnett walked slowly across the barroom and out the bat-wing doors, Stevens began to help Earl Beasely to his feet. "I would like to interview you, sir. My name is . . ."

Walking down the boardwalk to the sheriff's office, Dusty Barnett wondered how the scuffle in the saloon would read in the Philadelphia newspaper once Bradley Stevens embellished the facts to reach his "deeper, more profound truth."

Chapter Four

Phoebe Martin closed her script, turned off the kerosene lamp, quietly left her room, and walked outside of Martin's Restaurant. She didn't want to disturb her parents, who were both reading in the living quarters in the back. She had caused them enough trouble already.

She leaned against the outside wall of the restaurant, took in the stars, then bent over to pet the small friend who had followed her outside and been at her feet while she memorized her lines. "Why have you brought me here?" Phoebe whispered dramatically to the cat. "What horrid plans foster in your mild mind?"

Her face did a quick flinch. "No, no, that's not it." She took a deep sigh to calm herself, then spoke very carefully. "What horrid plans fester in your vile mind?" She smiled contentedly, then looked down at her friend. "It's not enough to just have the right words memorized, Horatio. The Lamonts told me that I need to speak my lines with conviction. Do you think I sounded as if I really felt the part?"

The cat brushed against the doorway, as footsteps sounded from across the road. Phoebe walked quickly to the opposite boardwalk as Horatio scampered quickly but cautiously beside her. "Clara Benson, you're as dependable as clockwork." As she spoke, Phoebe gently took a pitcher of lemonade from the elderly woman and began to walk beside her.

"Yes, this is the first Tuesday of the month." Clara laughed as she nodded at the basket of food she was carrying. "Harold will be working at the stage depot till midnight or near to it and has to eat in the office. But I don't think you will have to tote lemonade for me much longer."

"Oh?"

"That wonderful Mr. Connors didn't know much about the stagecoach business when he arrived, and Harold had to take on more responsibility. But Brett Connors is a smart young fellow! Harold told me that there would probably not be too many more of these late nights. . . ."

Phoebe Martin had grown up knowing Clara Benson and knew that the elderly woman was too polite to mention what she desperately wanted to talk about. Phoebe gave her an opening. "Clara, I sure don't mind carrying lemonade for you if you don't mind walking beside the most scandalous woman of Dawson, Arizona."

Clara's eyes took on new energy. "Only half the town thinks you are a scandal. The other half thinks you are wonderful. Without you, they couldn't see the play." The elderly woman's expression became intense, as if she were reviewing complex mathematical figures. "Of the ones who say you're a scandal, only about one third actually believe that. The rest are ladies who are jealous."

"What do *you* think, Clara?"

"Why, I think it's wonderful! I've never seen a play, and I'm running out of time. This could be the only chance I ever get." Clara paused for a moment, then became a bit bolder. "What does our town's deputy think about all this?"

Phoebe gave her companion a long sigh. "We talked about the play a few hours ago. He's not very happy with me."

The ladies stepped off one boardwalk and onto another. They were only a few stores away from the stage depot. "Well," Clara said, "you know how men are."

"Sometimes I'm not so sure that I do."

Two shots exploded from nearby. Phoebe dropped the pitcher of lemonade, spewing shards of glass and waves of liquid over the boardwalk. The cat darted into the night.

"That came from where my Harold is!" Clara's voice was a whispered terror.

A man emerged from the depot dressed entirely in black, including a cape and flat-brimmed hat. He ran to a black gelding tied to a hitch rail and crammed something into the saddlebags. The nightmarish figure quickly mounted, pulled out a gun, and fired into the air.

"The real phantom killer is here!" The shout came from behind a red mask and was loud, as if directed to the entire town. The intruder spurred the horse and galloped off.

"Oh, what—" Clara's entire body was trembling.

Phoebe tried to calm her friend. "This has to be a joke, Clara."

"Yes, yes."

"Stay here for a moment. I'll go look." Phoebe ran down the boardwalk. From out of the darkness, Horatio came running after her as if warning that what had happened was no joke. Together the young woman and her cat entered the stage depot. Clara's footsteps sounded from behind.

At first glance, the place looked almost tranquil. But it was the tranquility of the grave. Harold Benson's body lay in a widening pool of blood beside an open safe. Phoebe closed her eyes briefly as Clara Benson's scream filled the room.

Dusty Barnett stared intently at the black costume lying on the hotel bed. There were no signs that the outfit had been worn that night by a man who had ridden a horse.

"Now, is this the only phantom killer costume you have, Mr. Lamont?" Barnett had already done an informal search of the room.

"Yes, Sheriff. A theatrical troupe must travel light."

And can't afford duplicate costumes, Victor thought to himself as he spoke.

Victor and Jessica Lamont were standing at the foot of the bed in their hotel room. Beside them were Bert Lassiter and Charles Stafford. Dusty Barnett was standing on the left side of the bed along with Phoebe Martin and Caleb Hodge.

"And, Miss Martin, you are certain this is not the costume you saw the man who ran from the stage depot wearing?"

"I'm certain, Mr. Barnett. The man who killed Harold Benson had on an outfit very similar to this one, but the cape was smaller and made of thinner material. The black color wasn't as faded as the theatrical costume." Phoebe glanced quickly at the Lamonts as if embarrassed to have referred to their costume in an unflattering manner. She received kind smiles in response. The young woman then pointed at the scowling face that lay on the bed beside the costume. "The mask was much different. The killer was wearing a red bandanna with holes cut in it for the eyes and mouth. It was nothing at all like the mask." She seemed pleased to have made a positive comparison between the outfit worn by a killer and the theatrical costume.

Caleb Hodge eyed the Lamonts with contempt. "Now you say that all of you actors were at the church tonight getting ready for the play."

"That's right, Deputy," Victor Lamont replied politely. "We were rehearsing the scenes that didn't require

Connie Smith, the role that Miss Martin is playing. As soon as Miss Martin is ready, we will rehearse—"

"I don't think there should be any play! Not after tonight!"

Barnett noticed that neither one of the Lamonts displayed any anger at his deputy's outburst. Stafford and Lassiter looked irritated and impatient but not really angry. He reckoned that the actors were used to being treated with suspicion. "Much of the town saw the show last night," the sheriff said. "Wouldn't be any real trouble to make up a costume . . ." He looked directly at the Lamonts. "This play you are doing, does it get performed much? I mean, do lots of people know about it?"

"Well, sort of," Victor replied. "*The Phantom Killer* is a popular play, but I believe our troupe is the very first to perform it in the Arizona Territory."

"How about the mask?" Barnett nodded at the red face that scowled at him from the bed. "Do all the theatrical outfits that do the play use a mask like that one?"

"No," Lamont said in an almost jovial voice. "That mask represents a bit of good luck for the Lamont Theatrical Company. I bought it in California last year at a store run by a Mexican family. I'm not sure, but I think the mask was supposed to represent the devil. It was used for a festival of some kind."

Victor Lamont became increasingly relaxed. He seemed to enjoy talking about the small details of running a theatrical company. "You see, in the play, the phantom killer is the gardener who works at Winslow

Castle. His family was once rich and prominent, but most of them perished in a horrible fire. The ones who remain have to fend for themselves. Everything valuable was lost."

Barnett thought about that for a moment. "So, this gardener has gone a bit loco. He blames everyone for what happened to his family. He dresses up in a crazy outfit and runs around killing people and setting fires."

"Exactly!" Lamont spoke like a teacher addressing a student who had just performed well in class. "And he wears a black costume to symbolize death and a red mask to represent fire. Of course, every theatrical company has to come up with their own red mask." Lamont's chest swelled a bit. "I'll bet there's no company anywhere with a better mask than ours!"

"*The Phantom Killer* was written for a traveling troupe."

Dusty was a bit startled to hear Jessica Lamont talk. She had barely spoken since he arrived at the hotel with Phoebe and Caleb to inform the Lamonts about the murder of Harold Benson and the fact that he needed to talk with everyone in the troupe. Victor Lamont had immediately fetched the other two men from their room. Jessica Lamont had seemed to retreat into herself to the point that Barnett wondered if she really heard anything that was being said.

"Come again, ma'am?" Barnett smiled quizzically at the actress.

"*The Phantom Killer* was written for a traveling theatrical company." Jessica spoke in a charming, pleasant voice as if indulging in after dinner chitchat. "The play can be performed in a theater, of course, but it was written in such a way that it can be done in pantomime without any scenery. All that is really needed are costumes." She motioned toward a large, open trunk that contained all of the troupe's costumes, including that of the phantom killer. "The play has also been constructed in a manner that makes it possible for some of the actors and actresses to perform more than one part. *The Phantom Killer* was written for the strict economy that must be observed by a traveling troupe."

"Thank you, ma'am, and thank you, Mr. Lamont. I can sure use some education about the theater." *Not that I really want any,* Barnett thought to himself.

The sheriff was happy to get out of the Lamonts' room, but the walk down the flight of stairs in the hotel did nothing to relieve the tension of that evening. Caleb Hodge gave Phoebe Martin a hostile stare, which she ignored. The silence that followed made Barnett nervous to the point that he was almost glad to see Bradley Stevens waiting for them in the lobby.

"This will be on the front page of the *Philadelphia Tribune!*" Bradley proclaimed to the threesome.

"Good evening, Mr. Stevens." Barnett's cheer at seeing the reporter was already diminishing.

The reporter gave Phoebe a very appreciative smile. "You must be Miss Phoebe Martin."

"Yes."

"Could I interview you, Miss Martin? Oh, uh, my name is Bradley Stevens. I am not only a journalist but also the drama critic for my paper. I review—"

"I know who you are, Mr. Stevens. You are quite the talk of the town."

Bradley Stevens shrugged his shoulders in an elaborate gesture and tried to appear modest.

"Of course," Phoebe continued, "you are not the only one the chatterboxes in this town are gossiping about." Her voice and demeanor remained pleasant, which did nothing to improve Caleb Hodge's temperament.

But the reporter's temperament was improving at a gallop. "Miss Martin, I would be honored to escort you home. I find evening walks to be very pleasant, certainly preferable to riding on a horse. A stroll would give us a chance to talk."

"Why, yes, Mr. Stevens. If you could accompany me back to Martin's Restaurant, I would be happy to answer your questions along the way."

Bradley Stevens' eyes glowed as he strutted from the hotel beside Phoebe Martin. The two lawmen followed. The deputy's lips were pressed tightly together. He tried not to look at the couple but gave up on the notion and quickly glanced at them as he and Barnett crossed over to the opposite boardwalk.

"Why don't you wait a bit and then pay a visit on Miss Martin?" Barnett asked. "I know it's late to be calling, but she has had a very rough evening; first finding Harold Benson dead, then helping Doc Jamieson with Clara . . ."

"I've got nothing to say to her."

"Suit yourself."

Hodge remained quiet until they got to the sheriff's office, where he grabbed a Henry from the rack and announced that he was doing a round. The deputy's stride was almost a run as he exited the office, barely avoiding a collision with Reverend Colt.

The pastor closed the door and pointed behind him with a thumb. "What's wrong with that young man?"

"A young woman," Barnett replied.

"I should have known." The pastor smiled whimsically. "I guess it is a bit reassuring to know that even when the world seems to go crazy, certain things remain constant."

Barnett didn't really hear the remark. "You know, Reverend, Harold Benson's murder is even stranger than it seems."

"What do you mean?"

"There were bruises on his neck," Barnett explained. "Benson may have been strangled before he was shot. Harold was pretty frail—wouldn't have taken much to kill him."

"But why shoot a man who was already dead?" Reverend Colt's question led to a moment of uneasy silence, which the clergyman broke. "I've dropped by to deliver a bit of news, Sheriff." As Reverend Colt changed the subject, he fidgeted a bit, brushing back his frock coat and exposing the Colt that hung from his belt and was carefully tied down.

"Oh?"

"I received a telegram yesterday from an acquaintance in Boston—a preacher. He and his wife are coming out here to take over the Dawson Community Church. They should arrive in a few weeks. Of course, I'll stay until Harold Benson's killer is caught and all this phantom killer talk dies down, but then I'll be leaving. You're the only one I've told so far. I'd appreciate it if you'd keep it under your hat."

"Well, of course, Reverend, but why leave? You've been a real help to this town in the eight months or so that you've been here. I don't know what I would have done if you hadn't been around when those renegades were making their raids."

"That's over now, and I have a calling to answer."

"I don't follow you."

"My instructions come from the Bible. You remember that God wouldn't allow King David to build a temple. Before he became a king, David was a warrior. He shed a lot of blood. That made him unfit to build a house of worship."

Reverend Colt smiled sadly. "You're more polite than most folks in this town, Dusty. You've never asked me why I carry a gun. The answer is simple. I have killed some men, and now some men want to kill me." The pastor paused and then continued. "Like David, I am a man who has shed much blood upon the earth. Someone else will have to build the church."

Dusty Barnett looked confused. "But you did build the church! It was just finished about three months ago!"

"That's not really building a church." The pastor's sad smile returned. "That's just collecting wood and materials, which is what David did for the temple. Now the real building begins, or it will when that couple arrives from Boston."

"You will be missed, Paul."

"Thanks, Dusty. I'll miss you too." Paul Colten laughed in order to lighten the mood. "But, like I said, I'll stay until the phantom is caught." He moved toward the office door.

"I hope things go well for you, wherever you end up next."

"They will." The pastor's voice was light. "Remember, God didn't disapprove of David's being a warrior. David had a job to do—he committed violence so that others could live in peace. Guess that's my calling too." Reverend Colt pointed at the badge on Barnett's vest. "Of course, you know all about that." He moved a finger to his hat in a salute, then hastily left.

Dusty Barnett stepped from the office and stood outside the doorway, where he watched Reverend Colt disappear down the boardwalk. Colt was a tall man and fast with a gun. A man who naturally commanded respect. But he was also a restless man who preached some about peace but seemed to experience very little of it himself.

Barnett continued to watch the pastor as he gradually disappeared into the night. "God bless you, my friend," the lawman said quietly.

Chapter Five

The Fast Horse Saloon had been converted temporarily into a town hall. The round tables were stacked against the wall and replaced by rows of chairs. In the first row sat Reverend Colt, Dusty Barnett, Phoebe Martin, all of the members of the Lamont Theatrical Company, and Brett Connors. These were the people most likely to be asked questions.

Reverend Colt checked his pocket watch, returned it to his frock coat, and then stood up and faced the crowd. Barnett reflected sadly on the fact that no one in Dawson, except himself, knew that the town was about to lose an extraordinary man.

"Good evening!" Colt's deep voice silenced the chatter in the saloon. "The town council has asked me to ride herd on tonight's gathering. This meeting is being held to inform all of you about the murder that occurred last night in our town and to decide if, under the circumstances, the Lamont Theatrical Company should still present a play in Dawson on Saturday night."

The clergyman paused, and an iron firmness came into his eyes. "I wanted to hold this gathering in the church, but some of you thought it wrong to discuss such matters in a house of worship. I went along with that argument. But there are certain matters on which I will not compromise. This is an official town hall meeting. Ladies and children are present. There will be no swearing or rude behavior. We may be in a bar, but there will be no drinking until the meeting has concluded."

There was a murmur of comments and a few laughs. The pastor spoke over the din. "Sheriff Dusty Barnett will now summarize the events of last night."

Paul Colten sat down as Barnett stood up and did his best to give a clear, factual account of the murder that had occurred the previous night. He emphasized that the outfit worn by the killer was not the same costume that was used by the theatrical company. The sheriff explained that a little over four hundred dollars had been stolen from the safe in the stage depot. Much larger sums were kept at the depot at various times of the year, which might indicate that the killer knew little about the workings of the stagecoach company.

Barnett then opened the meeting to questions and was a bit astounded by the rumors that had been spread. All of the questioners referred to the murderer as the phantom killer, as if a character from a play had suddenly taken on real life and was running loose in the town. *Dawson needs a town newspaper to get facts to people quickly,* he thought. Then Barnett's eyes fell on Bradley

Stevens, who was frantically scribbling on a tablet, and the sheriff had second thoughts concerning that notion.

Barnett was explaining to one questioner that, as sheriff, he did not have the authority to declare plays, novels, or any other work of fiction to be illegal, when a familiar and unwelcome figure stepped through the bat-wing doors of the Fast Horse Saloon.

Cole Hayes viewed the proceedings with a cold indifference. Many years had passed since Barnett last saw that stare. Those years had not been kind to Cole Hayes. The gunfighter's face was gaunt, and a scar ran down his left cheek that had not been there when Barnett last saw him.

Hayes' gaze fell upon the sheriff, and Barnett thought he saw a brief glimmer of surprise followed by amusement. The gunfighter walked in a languid manner toward an empty chair in the back row and sat down. He casually tossed a cigarette stub from his mouth, crushed it underfoot, and began to roll another smoke.

When the questions were finished, Barnett returned to his seat in the front row. He wanted to sit somewhere else where he could keep an eye on Cole Hayes but decided that was a bad idea. Still, he hoped the meeting would be a short one.

Reverend Colt was again standing in front of the crowd. "We will now begin our discussion as to whether the play, *The Phantom Killer,* should be performed in Dawson. Mr. Victor Lamont, head of the Lamont Theatrical Company, has assured me that his people will be ready to perform the play this Saturday night. However, Mr. Lamont and his troupe sympathize with the town in the loss of one of our finest citizens and will abide by the decision that is made here tonight."

Raymond Dunning, a local cattle rancher, almost jumped to his feet. "This evil has got to be stopped!" Dunning was middle-aged and slim with salt-and-pepper hair. He waved his right arm as he spoke. "These theatrical people stand as guilty of the death of Harold Benson as if they had pulled the trigger themselves! They planted murderous thoughts in the mind of someone who made those thoughts a gruesome reality. An honest, law-abiding citizen is dead, and a church has been defiled! How many people will be murdered if this play is performed from beginning to end? These playactors should leave town immediately, and if they refuse, I say let's run them out of town!"

Raymond Dunning sat down to a smattering of applause and several shouts of approval. Those shouts began to gain momentum as Reverend Colt noticed a trembling hand being raised from a middle row.

"Quiet!" the clergyman shouted, and the voices diminished. "People will speak in turn, or they will not speak at all." Reverend Colt pointed in the direction of the quivering hand, and twelve-year-old Robbie Gosden stood up.

Robbie kept his eyes directly on the pastor as if afraid to look at the large room of people he was addressing. "Preacher, I am surely sorry about the death of

Mr. Harold Benson. He was a good man. I extend my sympathies to the widder."

Reverend Colt gave the boy an encouraging smile, and his nervousness subsided a bit. "But I sure do want to see that play. A play is somethin' special." The boy hurriedly looked at the people who surrounded him. "After seein' part of the play, I borrowed a book, *The Adventures of Tom Sawyer,* from the preacher. That's special too. I guess readin' that book is 'bout the nicest part of my day. Except, of course, for readin' the Good Book."

Robbie returned his gaze to the pastor. "Seein' the play will give us somethin' nice to think 'bout on those days when nothin' nice is happenin'." He stood silent for a moment, then blurted out a "thank you" and sat down.

Robbie's short speech blanketed the saloon with a sense of ease. There were no more shouts from the crowd. "Does anyone else wish to say something?" The pastor's question was answered with silence, and he called for a vote. A large majority of those present voted to allow the play to be performed. Reverend Colt ended the meeting with a short prayer. His eyes had only reopened for a few moments when Jessica Lamont approached him.

"Reverend Colt, that young man who just spoke—what is his full name?"

"Robbie Gosden."

"I must thank him."

"That would be nice, Mrs. Lamont."

"Oh, it is much more than just being nice, Reverend

Colt. People like Robbie, they are the reason—the justification, if you will—of why a theatrical company needs to exist." She smiled politely at the pastor, then headed in the direction of Robbie Gosden.

Several people began to crowd around the clergyman. He talked cordially with each one as he walked around to where he could see the actress chatting with the twelve-year-old boy. There was a look on the face of Robbie Gosden that would not appear often in the life of a lad raised on a struggling family ranch.

Reverend Colt had gone through a day of agonizing doubts about the wisdom of bringing a theatrical company to Dawson. Those doubts now vanished, and for a moment he felt peaceful and content.

"Good evening, Cole." Barnett stepped through the bat-wing doors of the Fast Horse and addressed Cole Hayes, who had just stepped off the boardwalk in front of the saloon.

Hayes stopped and turned around. "Well, well, Sheriff Dusty Barnett, still a small-town sheriff, workin' for small-town wages. Tell me, does that restaurant still give ya a free dinner on Sundays?"

Barnett nodded. "Folks like to show their gratitude."

Cole Hayes laughed mockingly. "Call it gratitude if ya like, but to me it sounds more like charity." A look of satisfaction filled the gunman's face as he saw the pain in Barnett's eyes. "I'll bet it takes six months of wearin' that piece of tin to make the money I get for one job."

"Why are you in town, Cole?" Barnett stepped off the boardwalk and stood beside the gunfighter.

"You're not bein' very friendly. Guess that talkin' 'bout money sort of puts you in an ornery mood." Hayes inhaled on his cigarette and blew a large puff of smoke in the lawman's direction. "Maybe we should change the subject to somethin' that'd make ya feel better, like fightin'. Remember how you bested me in that fight years back?"

"I remember."

"You whupped me good, in front of a gang I was ridin' with at the time. They had to ride me out of town in the back of a wagon. Took a couple of days before I could even walk straight for any decent amount of time. By then, the gang had all taken off on me. I lost their respect."

Barnett shrugged. "I guess that's a problem a man in your line of work just has to contend with."

"I got a question for you, Sheriff."

"Go ahead."

"Why did ya have to pound on me so hard? Ya had me beat good, but ya kept comin' on."

Barnett had not expected the question, which seemed to prick at something deep in his soul. He paused for some time before speaking. "Because you care nothing about human life, Cole. In your bank-robbing days you killed women and kids who just happened to be in the bank when you pulled the holdup. Nobody can prove it was you, but we both know it was. I wanted to show you that you can bring someone down good without using a gun."

"Never cared much for my methods, did you, Barnett?"

"Leave town at sunup, Hayes."

Cole Hayes laughed and spat on the ground to his right side. "Sheriff, I guess you've been a public servant so long, you kinda forgot what it's like in the business world." He stared directly into the eyes of the lawman. "If it's right for me, I'll leave tomorrow. Otherwise, you may have to learn about my methods all over again." The gunslick turned abruptly and walked away.

Chapter Six

Charles Stafford stepped out of the church and grinned as he saw the fancy carriage waiting for him. He winked at the pretty girl inside, who giggled in response.

"Father said that I could use his buggy but only for a couple of hours," the young woman said as Charles stepped up into the buggy and she scooted over to make room for him. "Father has to make calls on a few ranches this afternoon."

"That's no trouble at all, Miss Jamieson." Stafford took the reins with one hand and picked up a fine-handled whip with the other. He cracked the whip over two well-trained horses, who immediately began to move. "We don't have too long for lunch. I have to be back at the church this afternoon for more rehearsals."

"You actors certainly work hard." Her voice was a purr.

"Not many people realize that, Miss Jamieson. You're a lot smarter than most folks."

Crissy Jamieson looked down. "No, I'm not."

49

"Don't underestimate yourself, Miss Jamieson." As he spoke, Stafford noted that the carriage had a very comfortable seat. "You know, I consider myself lucky that some moron ran onto the stage and pushed me down before I had a chance to even know what was going on."

Crissy pointed ahead. "The road forms a *Y* pretty soon. Go to your left." She had spoken hastily, wanting to get back to the subject at hand. "Why are you happy that that terrible man shoved you?"

Stafford guided the horses as he had been instructed. "Why, otherwise, Dr. Jamieson would have had no reason to give me a quick once-over, and his beautiful daughter wouldn't have been holding that damp cloth over the bruise on my forehead. The moment I saw you, Miss Jamieson, I just knew that I was going to ask you to take a walk with me by the river."

Once again Crissy Jamieson looked down, and this time she was blushing. Charles Stafford mused at how easy all this was. He prided himself on never having to work hard at courting a gal. That sort of thing was for lesser men than himself.

"Stop right here by the tree."

As he halted the horses, Stafford quickly took in the terrain. The large tree provided a nice shade but not much in the way of privacy.

The actor hopped out of the carriage and scampered around to the passenger side of the buggy. Crissy handed him down a picnic basket with a large blanket draped across the top. Stafford took the basket and then held out a hand to help the young woman down. "Does your family picnic here often, Miss Jamieson?"

"Oh, yes. The old tree provides a wonderful shade. For really hot days there's the cave."

"The cave? Where's that?" Stafford cleared his throat, realizing he had been too quick with the question.

Crissy smiled demurely. "Why, up that hill." She nodded to her right. "It's a large cave. My father is over six feet, and he doesn't have to stoop to walk inside. The place is nice and perfectly safe. During the day there is plenty of light." Stafford followed the woman as she carried the basket under the tree and began to spread out the blanket. "My silly little brother, Sam, likes to make believe that there are mountain lions in that cave, as if the cave were somewhere up in the hills."

They both sat on the blanket. "You know, Miss Jamieson, this may sound a bit crazy, but I don't think I've ever been inside a cave."

When the first shot was fired, both of them looked around almost quizzically. "What was that?" Stafford blurted.

The second shot kicked up a spurt of ground near the blanket, and the couple scrambled to their feet, as a flock of birds exploded from out of the tree. "You little tramp!" Stafford yelled in a panic. "Why didn't you tell me you had a jealous boyfriend?"

"What do you mean?"

"Nobody would shoot at me! I've only been in town—"

A third shot went over their heads. Laughter and a horse's whinny could be heard from behind a nearby boulder.

Stafford grabbed the young woman by the arm. "Where did you say that cave was?"

Crissy pointed in the direction of the hill. Stafford landed a punch to her right eye and sent her sprawling onto the ground. The actor didn't want the girl following him.

"You can have her!" he shouted toward the boulder. Another shot was fired, this one landing close to Stafford's feet.

The actor ran toward the small hill and didn't break stride while going up the rocky incline. As he ran into the cave, he noted that the girl had been right. The first few yards were well lit by the sun. Charles stood still for a moment and listened. Approaching hoofbeats could be heard from outside. Maybe he should stay and confront the fellow directly—promise to stay away from Crissy. No, his pursuer was obviously in no mood for talk. Stafford ran into the darkness, hoping to find safety there.

He fell and plunged into mud. Water drops began to plunk onto his head, and a horrible laugh sounded from not too far away. Stafford started to get up as a voice boomed from near the entrance. "You get off this time, but the phantom will return." There was more laughter.

Stafford could hear retreating footsteps. A ploy,

maybe. Jealous boyfriends could pull some pretty strange tricks. Charles Stafford knew that from experience.

He remained still for several minutes, listening to the sound of his own breathing, then slowly rose and made his way back to the cave's entrance. He peered outside tentatively. There was nothing unusual. Apparently the boyfriend had taken off, content with having humiliated his rival. The fellow had probably seen the preview performance at the church yesterday and decided to do a bit of acting himself. Right now the guy was no doubt enjoying a good laugh.

Let him gloat, Charles Stafford thought as he walked slowly down the hill, examining his wet, dirty clothes. *There are plenty of other girls in town. That Phoebe gal who is playing Connie Smith in the play—she's more beautiful than Crissy Jamieson.* Phoebe had brushed off his initial attempts, but that just made it all the more interesting.

When he got back to the shady tree, Stafford dropped to the ground for a few moments of rest. As he had figured, the girl had driven off in her buggy. He would have to walk back to the church. Oh, well, a walk in the hot sun would dry his clothes.

After about ten minutes of not thinking or doing much of anything, the actor got back onto his feet and began to walk, figuring that it would be suppertime before he had a chance to get anything to eat.

The actor didn't know that he had an audience.

From a distance a man watched him with amusement while eating the fried chicken from Crissy's picnic basket. "Enjoy the day, Mr. Actor," he said. "It's going to be your last."

Chapter Seven

Sheriff Dusty Barnett carefully examined the bruise on Crissy Jamieson's face. "You say that Charles Stafford did this to you, Miss Jamieson?"

"He certainly did! Charles Stafford is a coward. He ran from the man who was firing at us and took refuge in the cave. He didn't want me to go with him."

"Why not?"

"Mr. Stafford had this crazy notion that the shooter was a jealous boyfriend I had jilted."

"Did you get a glance at the shooter?"

"No. After getting punched, I just stayed on the ground, trying to clear my head. I could hear a horse galloping off toward the cave, and a man yelled at me, 'Leave now, lady—the phantom will strike soon.'"

"And what did you do?"

"What do you think? I got into the buggy and left!"

"Sheriff, there is no need to continue this questioning any further. My daughter has already suffered through enough. You need to run those theater people out of our town immediately!"

Dusty Barnett scratched his head, more to collect his thoughts than to ease an itch. He was standing behind his desk surrounded by three Jamiesons: Hubert Jamieson, the town's only doctor; his wife, Millie; and, of course, their daughter, Crissy.

"I can't run the whole theatrical company out of town, Dr. Jamieson—you know that. But as soon as you file a complaint against Stafford—"

"We won't be doing that, Sheriff Barnett. No, we will not do that." Millie's voice broke just a bit as she spoke. Of the three Jamiesons present, she seemed to be having the hardest time keeping a calm composure.

Barnett's face and voice both expressed confusion. "Why not?"

Hubert Jamieson inhaled before he spoke. "Sheriff, we must consider Crissy's reputation. Our daughter had naturally sympathized with this Stafford fellow, who had been unfairly assaulted. He obviously planned to take advantage of her generous nature."

"There's more to it than that, Hubert." Millie's voice was a near whisper.

"Yes," the doctor continued. "Crissy will be leaving for the east soon to enter one of the few schools any-where that trains young women to become nurses. Nursing is a high, honorable calling, but there are many who regard nurses as women of low repute."

Barnett grimaced as a difficult memory flashed

through his mind. "Dr. Jamieson, during the War Between the States I spent two weeks in a medical tent. There was only one doctor around, and he had his hands full. But there were also two nurses, and those two ladies saved my life. I'll never say a bad thing about nurses."

The sheriff's remarks seemed to ease the tension in the office a bit. Barnett felt sorry for Hubert and Millie. From the gossip he had heard, Crissy's reputation in the town had been sullied for some time. Barnett thought that sending the girl east to school would be a disaster. Crissy didn't seem to have the inclination or desire to become a nurse. He hoped he was wrong.

Dusty Barnett returned to the point. "I'll have a talk with this Stafford fellow as well as the Lamonts, who own the theatrical company. I don't think Charles Stafford will be shooting off his mouth about Crissy or bothering her again in any way."

The doctor looked embarrassed. His gaze dropped to the floor, then returned to the lawman. "Thank you, Sheriff."

"I do have a favor to ask, Doctor."

"Yes?"

"Could you ask Sam to not play so hard when he comes over for a game of checkers? It's embarrassing to be whipped by a nine-year-old boy."

The remark brought some needed laughter. "That boy is a real pistol, isn't he?" the doctor said. There was more good-natured talk about young Sam as the Jamiesons left the office. As soon as they departed, the smile left Dusty

Barnett's face. He needed to talk with Stafford right away. Crissy had been right about one thing. That was no jilted boyfriend firing those bullets.

"Miss Smith, we have evidence that indicates that the Phantom Killer wants you as his next victim!"

"No! This cannot be!"

Charles Stafford, in his role as Dr. Philip Grayson, embraced Phoebe Martin. The hug was too long and too tight, in Phoebe's opinion. When he finally released her, Phoebe began to hastily spurt out a line. "Thank you—"

"No, Miss Dawson, Charles has the next line, then you come in."

"I'm sorry."

Victor Lamont and his wife both smiled from where they sat in the front pew. Victor Lamont spoke in a kind, friendly voice. "Don't get discouraged. After all, this is the first time we've rehearsed this scene. You'll do fine." He turned to the actor sitting behind him. "Let's take this scene from the top. Bert, get back up there."

Phoebe looked at the floor and sighed. Charles Stafford would get another embrace. She liked the Lamonts, but Stafford reminded her of a professional gambler—smooth and a bit too friendly, not someone you would ever trust. Well, at least he had changed his clothes from those dirty things he had returned in after lunch.

She felt more comfortable with Bert Lassiter, but he

seemed to be such a detached, sad man. He said and did very little when he wasn't acting, just sat alone, immersed in private thoughts. Earlier that morning Phoebe had been stunned by the energy Bert displayed when he was rehearsing. Apparently Bert Lassiter couldn't really exist without a script to tell him what to do and say.

The actor-director's voice pulled Phoebe from her musings. "Okay, Bert, we'll start with—"

The doors of the church opened. "Sorry, but I have to speak with Mr. Stafford." Dusty Barnett walked hastily to the front of the church.

Phoebe noted the frustrated looks on the faces of the actors. They obviously thought that this visit somehow concerned them—another intrusion of the law into their livelihood. But the young woman also spotted the serious expression on the face of the sheriff. This matter went far beyond a play.

"Of course, Sheriff." Victor Lamont stood up, and his voice sounded cordial, a concerned citizen eager to help the local law. "But why—"

"Someone took several shots at Mr. Stafford this afternoon while he was having a picnic lunch with Crissy Jamieson."

Victor looked stunned and angry. He looked up at Stafford, who was still standing beside Phoebe on the platform. "That's why your clothes were a mess. Why didn't you tell me about this?"

Charles Stafford shrugged. "We have a lot of work to

do here. Didn't want to slow things down." He wasn't a good enough actor to make those lines sound believable.

"Afraid I will have to slow things down right now," Barnett said. "Mr. Stafford, I'll need to talk with you for a few minutes. Let's go outside—we'll cause less disturbance there."

"Sorry, Sheriff, but—" Charles Stafford caught the look on his director's face. "Well, okay."

Barnett looked at the man standing beside him. "After I finish with Mr. Stafford, I'll need to jaw some with you."

"I figured as much." Lamont smiled but couldn't completely keep the weariness out of his voice.

The director watched the sheriff exit the church with the play's leading man, then addressed the remaining actors. "Okay, we'll back up a bit and do the scene where—"

"Mr. Lamont," Phoebe interrupted gently, "we need to take a moment for prayer."

"What the—" Lamont had heard many excuses from actors for delaying a rehearsal. This one was a first.

"We need to pray that the man responsible for shooting at Crissy and Charles is caught soon, before he harms somebody."

"Well . . ."

Jessica hastily stood up. "Yes, Phoebe, you are absolutely right. Would you please lead us?"

Victor bowed his head but didn't really hear Phoebe Martin's prayer. He had a vague respect for churchgoing people but wasn't a religious man and figured he probably never would be. But Victor Lamont knew one thing. If he did believe in prayer, he would now be praying for Saturday to come quickly, for the troupe to get through this one performance and leave the crazy town of Dawson forever.

Chapter Eight

Dusty Barnett moved quietly through the small grove of trees until he spotted his deputy, looking restless and unhappy. "Anything unusual happen?"

"No." Caleb Hodge glared at the church, which was about thirty-five yards in front of him. "That Bradley Stevens fellow showed up about an hour ago. Guess he's doing a story on how these playactors are trying to uplift us hayseeds." Hodge let out a deep breath as if trying to expunge the anger and frustration inside him. "Are you sure this Cole Hayes is going to try to kill Stafford to-night?"

Barnett nodded. "I've known Hayes for a long time. Everything about today fits his methods."

"You're sure that was him taking the shots at Crissy and the actor?"

"Positive. That's Cole Hayes' style. He likes to toy with his victims before killing them. Everyone in town is talking about *The Phantom Killer.* He would have heard enough about the play to have his own kind of fun with it."

"But why kill Stafford?"

"I talked some with Victor Lamont. Seems that Stafford has a reputation as a ladies' man. He joined the troupe in Denver and was anxious to leave town. My guess runs that he broke the heart of a young lady with a rich daddy who hired a gunman to avenge his daughter's honor."

"You said something earlier about talking with Stafford. . . ."

"That didn't go too well. The actor is convinced that what happened this afternoon was the work of a jealous boyfriend, nothing else."

A loud shout followed by raucous noise emanated from the church. The actors were obviously rehearsing an action scene. "Sure be glad when all this tomfoolery is over." Anger laced Caleb's voice and stayed there as he asked, "You're positive that Hayes will make his move tonight?"

"Cole doesn't stay in one place long. He's had his fun. Now he'll wait until Stafford is alone, but if he can't do it that way, then he'll kill Stafford and anyone else who is a witness." Dusty's eyes scanned the wooded area behind the church. "He's out there someplace, and he knows that I'm trying to stop him."

"Guess we got no choice but to just stay close to Stafford." Caleb's gaze fell to the ground, then went back to Barnett. "Why didn't you just run Hayes out of town?"

"That's what I should have done," the sheriff answered. "But Hayes would have taken a stand on it, and it seemed wrong to kill a man because he wouldn't leave town."

A look of understanding washed over Caleb's face. The sheriff was happy to see it there. His deputy considered killing a very serious matter.

"I'll take over," the sheriff continued. "Why don't you get back to the office? Reverend Colt is there right now. Of course, I'm sure he wouldn't mind staying on the job a bit longer if you want to stop at the church and walk Phoebe home."

Caleb Hodge's lips turned thin. Several awkward moments passed before he spoke. "No need in keeping the reverend any longer than need be." He took a last quick look at the church, then headed for the office.

Twenty minutes later the sheriff thought it a good thing that Caleb had not tried to see Phoebe. The young lady departed from the church with Bradley Stevens, who was obviously escorting her home.

Dusty Barnett was certain that Phoebe had no serious interest in the reporter. But Bradley Stevens represented a glamorous world, which Phoebe, in a way, had entered. A chagrined look cut across the sheriff's face. Of course, there was likely more to it than that. Caleb had, no doubt, said some pretty stupid things to the young woman after he found out that she was going to be in a play. Phoebe was hurt and striking back at the man who had inflicted the wound.

The rest of the crew followed Phoebe and Bradley out the door. They all began walking into town. Barnett had no trouble following, unnoticed, from a distance.

Phoebe and Bradley headed in the direction of the restaurant, while the other actors headed for the hotel. But Charles Stafford said good night to his companions at the hotel and continued walking to the Golden Nugget Saloon.

As the sheriff walked slowly by the Golden Nugget and glanced inside, he wondered, casually, if Cole Hayes hadn't been following *him*. Dusty found the notion amusing. He and the gunfighter had one big thing in common on this night. They were both men with an important job to do. Hayes had been paid to kill a man now staying in Dawson, and Barnett was paid to protect the denizens of the town.

The lawman stopped and looked around. There was nothing to be concerned about, just the usual rowdies making a loud rattle against the vast indifference of the night.

"Well, well, good to see that our sheriff is keeping an eye on this establishment of dubious reputation." A portly man of medium height stepped through the Golden Nugget's bat-wing doors and onto the boardwalk. His voice carried a tinge of mockery.

"Hello, Jordan." Barnett tried to appear happy to see the man. "I guess you're in town for your weekly poker game."

"Yes, I am, Sheriff." Jordan Myers wasn't drunk, but there was more than a whiff of alcohol on his breath. "And, I must say, lady luck was very kind to me tonight."

"Glad to hear it."

Jordan Myers laughed as if brushing off the lawman's last statement. "Well, you'll have to excuse me, Sheriff. I need to get home to the little lady." He winked in a lewd manner, then mounted his bay, which was tied to the hitching rail in front of the saloon, and rode off.

Dusty Barnett sighed and quietly entered the Golden Nugget. He exchanged friendly words with several patrons as he made his way across the saloon. He positioned himself near the left end of the bar, where he could easily see Charles Stafford, who was engaged in a poker game.

"A beer, Sheriff?" the bartender called out from opposite end of the bar, where he was serving two customers.

"Yeah, Pat, no hurry."

But in short order Pat Nolan, who owned, in his words, "a chunk of the Nugget," was setting a mug in front of the lawman and shaking his head as Dusty started to lay some money on the bar. "It's on the house, Sheriff."

"No, let me—"

"It's the least I can do." Pat was a young, muscular

man with reddish brown hair. "I appreciate the way you uphold the law in Dawson. You deserve an occasional free beer. Besides—" He dropped his voice to a whisper. "I know how little this stingy town pays you." He gave Dusty a friendly laugh, then hurried off to tend to other customers.

Barnett took a sip of his beer and fought the depression building inside him. Pat's "stingy town" remark was well-intentioned, but it came at a bad time.

Dusty Barnett allowed himself a mental foray into the past. He had been sheriff of Dawson for two years when he met and fell in love with Marietta Cummings. He had had a rival for Marietta's affections, Jordan Myers, who was a year or so away from taking over the family ranch from his father.

This time, the sheriff took more than a sip from his mug. The craziest mistake he'd ever made was on the night of that horrible day when he killed two boozed-up cowboys who were rampaging across town, firing at whoever came into their sight. They had wounded three people when the sheriff took them down. As he crouched over the dead bodies, he realized that one of them couldn't have been more than fifteen.

That evening he'd sat in Marietta's parlor and tried to explain to her the horrible pain he carried inside. Looking back on it, he had to admit that he was looking for Marietta to tell him that what he'd done was right and necessary. He wanted comfort and sympathy.

The woman didn't have any of that. "Dustin, your job

is so terrible. And, well, my father is on the city council, and I know how little they pay you. . . ."

Barnett was stunned. The lawman hadn't expected this reaction from the woman he loved. He suddenly felt embarrassed for having dumped his problems onto her. He must have appeared as a weakling in her eyes. The sheriff just nodded his head as Marietta spoke about the need for him to turn in his badge and find more profitable employment. He'd left as soon as he could.

The next morning he awoke with a sense of urgency. He knew he had to find a way to explain to Marietta why it was important for him to remain an enforcer of the law. It wouldn't be easy, but he would wait a few days and then give it a try.

Barnett glanced at Charles Stafford. The actor seemed to be losing at cards. The sheriff fiddled with his mug, then took another drink as his mind again returned to the past.

Eleven days went by before he had a chance to speak with Marietta. Two days after his disastrous meeting with her, the bank was robbed, and it took over a week for Barnett to catch up with the crooks and bring them in along with the money.

He had spotted the young woman coming out of the general store. He took off his hat as he approached her and invited her to have dinner at Martin's Restaurant that evening.

What followed next remained fixed forever in Barnett's mind. Marietta looked away for a moment, then looked back at Barnett. There was a melancholy in her face, but she managed to smile. "Dustin, you are a fine man, and I have very much appreciated the time we have had together. But while you were gone, there were some changes in my life. Mr. Jordan Myers has asked me to be his wife, and I have accepted."

Charles Stafford was still losing at cards. Dusty Barnett laughed quietly, but he was laughing at himself, not the actor. On that day the lawman had, somehow, managed to say all the right things, but his thoughts were far from proper. The woman was marrying a selfish lout, and she'd spend the rest of her life in misery, mourning the lost opportunity of marrying a fine man like Dustin Barnett.

The sheriff smirked and rubbed the back of his neck. It sure hadn't turned out that way. Mrs. Marietta Myers was, by all evidence, a very happy woman who was living a life that he never could have given her. And she was still beautiful. Four kids, six grandkids, and the passage of many years hadn't changed that. Every time he saw her in town, he still felt—

Stafford tossed in his cards, pushed back his chair, and left the saloon in a huff. Not wanting to look too conspicuous about following the actor, Dusty Barnett took a final sip of his beer and ambled out of the Golden Nugget. Outside, he looked about hurriedly. Stafford had vanished. The sheriff cursed under his breath and walked briskly in the direction of the hotel, then ran down the first alley he came to. He stopped at the back of a feed-

and-grain store and listened. From a distance he could hear frantic sounds, like a terrified baby crying for help. More likely it was Charles Stafford pleading with his captor through a gagged mouth.

The sound receded into the distance, and Barnett followed it. He moved quickly while not making too much noise. Cole Hayes was probably expecting him, but there was no sense in sounding a trumpet before he arrived.

"I'm puttin' you out with the trash, Mr. Actor." The voice belonged to Hayes, and what he said made sense. Near the edge of town there was a trail that led into the woods and a clearing that was used as a dump. The spot was far enough away that a gunshot wouldn't cause much attention in the town, and it would be well into the next day before anyone found the body.

The trail was wide, and darkness provided the sheriff with sufficient cover as he followed the gunfighter and his captive. When they came to the dump, Hayes pushed Stafford to the ground. "Ya know, I've never been a churchgoin' man, but I do remember one time I was in church, trailin' a man I would kill that night. Well, the preacher talked about a fella named Job. Seems that all sorts of bad things happened to this Job, and he ended up on a heap of ashes, where he had to listen to a bunch of fools tellin' him how he did wrong."

Hayes began to laugh as Barnett moved in and ducked behind a tree, where he could get a good view provided

by the bright moon. Stafford was indeed lying on a pile
of ashes, with Hayes crouching over him. The actor was
gagged with his hands tied behind him. He twitched
helplessly as Cole Hayes wrapped a rope around his
ankles. At the left side of the ashes stood a monstrous
contraption with an arm that seemed to merge with the
surrounding darkness. Giving it a second glance, Barnett recognized the beast as an old potbellied stove. He
had remembered hearing a lady tell Phoebe in Martin's
Restaurant, "I'm going to have my husband put that old
stove of ours in the dump, where someone who truly
needs it can take it without the embarrassment of ac-
cepting charity."

Apparently no one truly needed it.

Hayes stopped laughing, but his voice still rang with
amusement. "Well, Mr. Actor, you're not gonna hafta
listen to a bunch of fools. No, sir, I'm gonna take care
of that right now."

"The Sunday school lesson is over, Cole." Barnett
spoke as he walked briskly toward the gunman and his
captive.

"Well, well, Dusty, I've been sorta half expectin' ya."
Hayes' voice and demeanor were casual, but the ember
at the end of his cigarette flared up. The gunfighter was
breathing faster.

"Take off your gun, and drop it to the ground, Cole."

Hayes paused for a moment; the ember on his smoke
drooped and flamed to the ground. Barnett recalled that

he had never seen Cole without a cigarette dangling from one side of his mouth and remembered why he had given up smokes years before.

The gunslick tossed away the stub of his cigarette, spit, then smiled at his opponent. He took in Barnett's straight posture and steady hands. He figured that those hands hadn't slowed much. "Why, sure, I'll take off my gun. Only why don'tcha join me?"

"What do you mean?"

"How long has it been since you whupped me good in that fight, Dusty?"

"Oh, five years."

"More like eight, I'd say."

"Could be."

"Dusty, you say you never cared much for my methods. You claim to be a man who don't like killin'." Hayes slowly moved his hands to the buckle of his gun belt. "So let's take off our guns and settle this matter with fists. You win, then I end up in jail. I win, then I get on my horse and leave town without hurtin' a soul. How does that sound?"

Barnett knew it was a trap. Hayes was about fifteen years younger than he and wanted to exploit it. If the outlaw could down the lawman in a fistfight, he would grab a gun and finish him for good, then put a bullet into Charles Stafford.

"Untie the actor, Cole. Then maybe we can talk terms."

"He'll go for help."

"No, he won't." Barnett was certain that he was speaking the truth. "Once he is out of it, Stafford doesn't care what happens to either one of us. Besides, the man is a coward. He hit a woman earlier today. Of course, you know all about that."

"Guess I do. But I'm a businessman bein' paid good money to kill this piece of trash by the father of a girl he, well, took advantage of."

"You're not making a penny in this town, Cole. The best you can hope for is that I'll take you up on that offer of a fistfight. That way you may be able to ride out of town with a lot of bruises instead of resting in the grave-yard, which is where you know I'd put you in a gunfight."

Anger flared in the gunfighter's eyes. He bent over and untied the ropes binding the actor. "Barnett, I'll just give up this job for the pleasure of a little revenge. I haven't forgotten that beating you gave me. And you're not going to forget the one I give you tonight."

Charles Stafford struggled to his feet and untied the gag around his mouth. Barnett motioned with his head for the actor to take off. The gesture was unnecessary. Stafford hurriedly scrambled into the woods. There the sheriff knew that Charles Stafford would watch the fight. If Barnett won, Stafford would return to the hotel and not mention the incident to anyone. Why do further damage to his reputation with a story about an angry father seeking revenge? If Hayes won, the actor would leave town quickly.

Cole Hayes now stood directly facing Dusty Barnett

with his hands once again on his gun belt. Barnett was tempted to go for his gun. He was certain that he could outdraw Hayes. But, somehow, that seemed wrong. Dusty Barnett placed his hands on the buckle of his gun belt, and, simultaneously, both men took off their guns, dropped them to the ground, and scooted them to the side with their feet.

Cole Hayes advanced with remarkable speed on the sheriff and threw a fast barrage of punches. Barnett ducked all of them but had to move quickly to do so, which had been Cole's strategy. He wanted to wear the older man down.

Hayes delivered a hard right, which Barnett couldn't completely duck; it landed above his left ear. The lawman staggered backward.

Cole looked about to see if he could grab a gun before his opponent recovered. Barnett took advantage of the brief opening, lurched forward, and swung a hard right, which broke the nose of Cole Hayes.

The gunfighter stumbled backwards, and a light, crackling sound whiffed as Hayes backed into the ash heap. Barnett slowly stalked in after him, and the two men circled each other.

Hayes unleashed another brutal array of punches in the vicinity of Barnett's head. Dusty moved up his arms to block the onslaught, and Hayes delivered a hard kick to Barnett's right knee. The lawman plunged into the ashes, sending up a black cloud.

His nose spurting blood, Hayes ran to his gun belt and

retrieved the pistol. Feeling confident with the gun in his hand, Cole waded back into the ashes until he reached the cloud that was now settling back down on the lawman.

"Dusty, looks like—" Hayes began to cough. "See what ya done? Got all that ash dust in my throat." Mockery laced Cole's voice.

"That isn't dust, Cole."

"What do you mean?"

"All those cigarettes you smoke, Cole. They can do mean things to a man's insides." Barnett slammed a foot into the gunfighter's chest. The gun flew from his hand, and Hayes again stumbled backward, this time coughing viciously.

The gunman plowed into the potbellied stove, breaking off the pipe, which landed beside him as he dropped to the ground. Hayes saw a shadow coming toward him. Dusty Barnett was back on his feet.

Hayes scrambled up, grabbed the pipe, and swung it at Barnett, flinging soot into the air. But his opponent had moved in too close. Barnett landed three quick punches to the head, sending his opponent back into the ashes. The gunfighter didn't realize it, but the force behind those punches almost caused Dusty Barnett to lose his balance. But the sheriff, taking fast gulps of breath, managed to stay upright.

"You win, Barnett. You win." Hayes gently touched his broken nose, then sat up. "Shoulda known I couldn't take you in a fight."

"Raise your hands, Cole. Right now."

"Anything you say," the outlaw wheezed. "Just give me a minute to catch my breath."

With a speed of hand that any gambler would envy, Hayes drew a Butterfield .41 caliber pocket pistol from his boot. Barnett had anticipated the move and kicked the weapon from the gunfighter's hand. The sheriff staggered in the direction of where the Butterfield had hit the ashes and quickly retrieved it.

"Okay, Cole, you're going to get back on your feet very slowly, keeping your hands away from your body the whole time."

The gunman did what he was told, and the two men were once again looking at each other, eye to eye.

"You're right, Cole. I never did care much for your methods." Barnett lifted the .41 that he had pointed at Hayes. "Good thing I never forgot them."

Chapter Nine

Dusty Barnett felt nervous as he walked toward the stage depot. He tried to tell himself there was no reason to feel that way. Amos Martin was a good man who could keep a confidence. But Amos was also an observant man who would certainly wonder what was going on if the sheriff of Dawson came even close to asking him to encourage his daughter to patch things up with Deputy Caleb Hodge.

Barnett wondered why it was so important to him that Caleb and Phoebe get back together. Although he felt uneasy admitting it, he supposed that he did regard Caleb as a son. He had watched Caleb grow up and had started taking the boy hunting after his father, a good friend, died.

But it went even further than that. Phoebe reminded him a bit of Marietta when she had been a very young woman and he was courting her. But, in many ways, Phoebe was different than Marietta. Phoebe was more of a churchgoing woman who had been a real help in organizing various events for Reverend Colt. She could handle being a lawman's wife, low pay and everything else.

Dusty Barnett knew that being the sheriff of Dawson was his calling. He had no regrets about giving more than twenty years of his life to the job. But loneliness had plagued him throughout, and he wanted better for Caleb.

As the sheriff entered the depot, Amos was sitting at a desk, making entries in a ledger. "Good to see you, Dusty, but you came at the wrong time. Brett ain't nowheres about."

"I came to see you, Amos, if you can spare me the time."

The old man laughed amicably. "Do me good to jaw for a spell. Between workin' at my restaurant and doin' poor Harold Benson's job, I ain't had much time for socializin'."

"Brett Connors tells me he couldn't be running the place without you right now." Barnett sat down in a chair beside the desk.

"At my age, you take any compliment you can get. But I won't be doin' this here job much longer. Brett is bringin' in a chum of his from back east to take over Harold's job. I'll be able to get back to just runnin' my restaurant along with Amelia, my overworked wife, and Phoebe, my actress daughter. Listen to me kick! You're the one who's been busy. From what I hear tell, you jailed a famous outlaw last night."

"Yeah, found out this morning that he's wanted for murder in Tucson. A U.S. Marshal will be arriving tomorrow to take him away. The good citizens of Dawson won't have to pay to feed Cole Hayes for very long."

"Good thing." Amos chuckled. "Now I guess you got to find the fella who put on that crazy costume and murdered Harold Benson."

Barnett smiled at the old man. "I thought maybe you could help me out a bit with that job."

"I don't follow you, Dusty."

"I didn't know Harold Benson too well. I got along with him, but our paths just didn't seem to cross all that much. You and Amelia were close friends with the Bensons. What can you tell me about Harold?"

Amos Martin looked up at the ceiling for a moment, then eyed his companion. "Loyal. That's the word that best sums up Harold. When Harold Benson became your friend, you had a friend for life, through thick or thin."

"Did that loyalty apply to his job?"

"You betcha." Amos pointed to a portrait of a distinguished-looking gentleman that hung on the wall behind him. "That's Thaddeus Connors. He and his wife, Abigail, came to this town right after the war. By jimminy, must have been sixty-six. That was a bit before your time, wasn't it?"

"Yes, I arrived a year or so later," Dusty nodded at the portrait. "I knew that was Thaddeus, but I never met him or any member of the Connors family until, of course, Brett arrived."

"Thaddeus didn't stay in Dawson long, but he didn't let any grass grow under his feet while he was here. He set up this stage depot and put his younger brother, Louis, in charge and hired Harold to keep the books and generally look after the place. Then he and the missus went back east."

"Sounds to me like Thaddeus didn't have much confidence in his brother."

Amos gave a whimsical laugh. "No, he didn't. You remember how Louis was—a nice enough sort but lazy. I guess his big brother was the hard worker in the family. But it went okay. Harold pretty much ran the depot and got paid good to do it. Every month Harold would write a letter to Thaddeus, tellin' him what was goin' on, and Thaddeus would write him back. Thaddeus died two years or so ago, and Harold would write his reports to the widow, Abigail."

Barnett took a moment to reflect on what he had just been told. "When Louis Connors died, why didn't the family just put Harold in charge of this depot?"

Amos made a steeple with his hands. "I think Harold kinda got his feelin's hurt because they didn't. But he understood. Blood is thicker than water and all that. Apparently Brett wasn't doin' too good in the east, and the family figured that a move west would make a man of him. And that's what happened."

"So, Harold remained loyal to the Connors family?"

"Sure enough did! Why, a letter arrived here for

Harold from the widow Abigail just yesterday. Brett was here, and we opened it together. Abigail thanked Harold for helping her youngest nephew and said that the family portrait he asked for was on the way—not a paintin', mind you, but a real picture! Guess Harold planned to hang it up beside the portrait of Thaddeus."

"Did Harold keep the letters he received from Abigail?" The excitement in his voice surprised Barnett.

"Sure." Amos pointed downward. "Just like Harold. He's got those letters neatly stacked and arranged by year in the bottom drawer."

"May I see the letters from this year?"

"Don't see why not." Amos Martin pulled open the drawer and handed Barnett eight letters.

The sheriff stared at the papers in his hand for a few moments, as if there was some secret hidden there, waiting to be uncovered. "Amos, from what you have seen, is there any sign at all that, well, that things aren't what they should be with the stage depot?"

"You don't suspect Brett Connors of doin' somethin' wrong do you, Dusty?"

Barnett shrugged his shoulders and looked embarrassed. "I'm just a lawdog, sniffing around trying to find a trail that leads somewhere. Harold knew everything about this business, and, well—"

The old man waved his right hand back and forth. "I gotcha, I gotcha. You got a job to do." He stopped waving and gave the sheriff a comforting smile. "But I can tell you, the books here are in perfect order. Not one penny unaccounted for."

A look of relief washed over the sheriff's face. "Thanks, Amos. I had to ask. . . ."

"I know—what we're sayin' here is just between you, me, and Thaddeus." The old man again pointed to the portrait on the wall.

Barnett smiled, then hesitated. He didn't want to bring up the next topic but felt that he owed it to Amos Martin. "You know, Amos, this play that Phoebe is in, it has some folks who should know better braying like donkeys. I hope you're not letting some of the stuff that is being said about your daughter get to you. She's . . . well . . . she's a very fine lady."

Amos Martin's eyes appeared to get a bit moist, and his voice dropped to a whisper. "Thanks, Dusty. Phoebe knows what a lot of folks don't. The west is changin'. Slowly, maybe, but it is changin'. Someday, I hope, everyone in this town will be able to read. Maybe we'll have ourselves a library here, just like they do in the big cities. And, yeah, maybe even a theater." The old man laughed as if mocking his own seriousness. "I won't live to see that day. But maybe Phoebe will."

"Phoebe's got a fine head on her shoulders—in every way. Just hope she can forgive some of the things Caleb has said to her of late."

Amos Martin gave the sheriff a comforting smile. "They'll work it out, Dusty."

As he left the stage depot, Dusty Barnett suspected that his friend understood him better that he had thought. The lawman also hoped that Amos was right about Dawson, Arizona, someday boasting a library and theater. Yet he couldn't be completely at ease with having a play performed in the town. A play seemed to do sort of crazy things to folks. Maybe it was just as well that he was turning in his star. The world seemed to be changing, and he wasn't sure that he could keep up with it.

Barnett laughed out loud at his musings. The town didn't pay him to be a philosopher. He still had a job to do. Dusty Barnett quickened his pace as he headed for the sheriff's office.

Chapter Ten

Leonard Behan lay the Henry .44 down on the counter of the store and tapped his hand on it affectionately as if he were patting the head of a grandson. "Doesn't need too much work. I can have it for you the day after tomorrow. Is that okay, Sheriff?"

"Sure, Len. It's one of the rifles we keep in the rack at the office. There's no rush." Barnett rested his elbows comfortably on the counter of Behan's Gun Shop, which, conveniently enough, was right across the street from the sheriff's office.

"You know, I could have had it for you sooner, but the stiffness in my hands is getting worse—what's that fancy word Doc Jamieson has for it?"

"Arthritis."

"Yeah, it's slowing me down. Say, I haven't told anyone about you buying the store and all. Still think you can take over in six months?"

Barnett nodded, but his face expressed a touch of doubt. "Appreciate your keeping quiet about it, Len. Yes,

I think so. The next election for sheriff is in five months. Caleb shouldn't have any trouble getting elected."

"And if the young 'un has any problems being sheriff, why, all he'll have to do is cross the street, and you'll be right here."

Barnett smiled as he took his elbows off the counter. "Yes, guess I'll always be a lawdog. Only in six months I'll be a volunteer deputy."

"You don't fool me one bit, Sheriff. You'll be an old warhorse who charges every time at the smell of smoke. Say, how 'bout the town council?"

"What about it?"

"Why not run to take my place on the council? I don't want to do it no mores, and you'd be a shoo-in."

"And as a member of the council, I'd have a say in how much the new sheriff gets paid. Sounds like a good idea, Len."

The two men shared a laugh as Barnett left the shop. Closing the door behind him, the lawman could see a boy across the street anxiously looking into the window of the sheriff's office.

"Over here, Robbie!"

Robbie Gosden ran across the street to the front of Behan's Gun Shop. "My boss, Mr. Pat Nolan, sent me to git you, Sheriff."

"Why?"

"Mr. Nolan says it's nothin' urgent. There's no fights at the saloon—nothin' like that. Still, he needs to jaw with you soon."

"Thanks, Robbie. I'll get right over there."

"Uh, Sheriff?"

"Yes."

"Mr. Nolan won't get in no trouble, will he? I mean, I know it's wrong for me to be workin' at a place like the Golden Nugget, or that's what some folks say, but if it weren't for the money I get sweepin' floors, stackin' and all, our family wouldn't—"

"There's no problem, Robbie. In the west we can't get ourselves too worked up over matters like that. We got too many real troubles to worry about."

The boy relaxed a bit. "Thanks, Sheriff."

"Are you finished at the Golden Nugget for today?"

"Yes, sir."

"Then run along. Your folks will be looking for you."

Run along he did. Robbie ran swiftly and gracefully toward the Golden Nugget, where his horse was tethered. Dusty Barnett stood and watched the boy for a minute, musing that, at the age of twelve, you ran just about everywhere.

But at forty-nine, the sheriff was content with a brisk walk.

Chapter Eleven

As he entered the Golden Nugget, Barnett immediately spotted the owner of the saloon, who was tending bar.

"What's going on, Pat?"

"Maybe nothing." Pat looked about in a fidgety manner. "Maybe I shouldn't have sent for you. . . ."

"Don't worry, your judgment is good. Tell me what's bothering you."

Nolan cut his eyes toward the left. "The Gavens brothers, Blaine and Jeb—they've been jawing about hanging Cole Hayes. Right now it's just a lot of talk, but, later, after they've had more whiskey. . . ."

"Thanks." The lawman nodded at Nolan, then walked to the table where the Gavens brothers were drinking and laughing with four other men. Blaine's voice could be heard above the rest. "I'll bet that reporter fella from Philadelphia would write about us. We'd be heroes back east."

"Maybe not," one of his companions said jokingly.

"Why, he might tell them easterners that we're jus' cold-blooded killers."

"So what?" Blaine yelled back. "We'd still get our names in the newspaper!"

They broke into raucous laughter that quickly subsided as Dusty Barnett approached their table. "Evening, gentlemen."

"Evenin', Sheriff," Blaine Gavens said with mock cordiality. He was a burly, bald-headed man with a half ring of black hair that ran from one ear to the other. "Nice of you to stop by and be sociable."

"I hope being sociable is all you gents have in mind for tonight."

"Why, we've been thinkin' about our civic duty." Jeb Gavens spoke up. He was smaller than his brother and several years younger with thick black hair and a well-groomed mustache. Barnett wondered, casually, if Jeb took good care of his hair as a way of topping his big brother.

"We good citizens might decide to do the law a favor and hang that gunfighter you've got in the jail," Jeb continued. "No sense in goin' through all that trouble and expense to bring a circuit judge here. The whole world knows that Cole Hayes has killed a lot of men in cold blood."

"And we'll make this town famous!" Blaine again shouted, as if wanting to grab back attention from his younger brother. "That Stevens dandy will put us on the front page of the newspaper in Philadelphia!"

Dusty Barnett spoke in a low monotone. "If you try to hang anyone, you could end up dead. And it won't be on the front page of the Philadelphia paper or any other paper. Nobody is going to care much what happens to you jaspers."

The lawman walked slowly back to the bar. "Thanks again for letting me know what's going on, Pat. I'm obliged."

"Do you think they'll really try anything, Sheriff?"

Barnett glanced over the bat-wing doors at the large red patch in the sky. "They'll need more darkness and more liquor, but, yeah, there's going to be trouble."

Barnett turned and faced Nolan directly. "Think maybe you can help us out tonight?"

"Sure can. Isaac should be here in about an hour. He can take over the bar. I'll strap on a gun and get over to your office."

"I appreciate your volunteering, Pat. You used to wear a badge, didn't you?"

A wistful look came over the bar owner's face. "Yeah, back in Texas I was a deputy for a while. Enjoyed doing it. Enjoyed it a lot, as a matter of fact. But I'm a man who also enjoys the feel of money in his pockets. That feeling never comes to you when you wear a tin star. Still, I'm grateful for men like you, Sheriff, who look at things a bit differently. You know, if it wasn't for good lawmen like you, men like me could never wear themselves out trying to get rich. I'm happy to help you anytime, Dusty."

Dusty Barnett saluted the bar owner with two fingers

to his hat, then slowly left the saloon. Partway through the bat-wing doors he glanced back at the Gavens brothers, who were pouring themselves drinks. The sky was still the color of blood.

Knowing that he would have to stay close to his prisoner that night, Barnett decided to do a round before returning to the office. The sheriff's round, as usual, extended to the Dawson Community Church. He planned to walk around the wooden building and then head back. As he reached one side of the church, he heard Phoebe Martin's voice.

"Dr. Grayson, had it not been for your quick thinking and noble courage, I would still be in the clutches of that horrible fiend."

The sheriff stopped. Phoebe was obviously behind the church, going over her lines for the play. Barnett reckoned that he didn't really need to walk around the building. He had turned and taken a few steps away when Phoebe's voice again came at him. "That's enough, Mr. Stafford!"

Phoebe's warning was followed by male laughter. "Come on now, you want our romantic scenes to be convincing, don't you?"

The sheriff decided to walk around the building after all. As he turned the corner, Phoebe was prying Charles Stafford's hand from her arm. "I'm not telling you again—"

"Let her go, Stafford, right now!"

The actor released Phoebe and looked at the new-comer with contempt. "This is none of your business, Sheriff."

"Get back into the church, Stafford. And keep your hands off Miss Martin, or you'll regret it."

Stafford laughed once again, but the laugh was forced and hollow. "You obviously know nothing about the theater! Miss Martin and I have to rehearse—"

"Rehearse all you need to," Barnett said. "But I'm telling Lamont that you are not to be left alone with Miss Martin. Now move."

Anger and humiliation contorted Charles Stafford's face. He took two steps toward the lawman. "We're taking a break. I like the air right here just fine."

Barnett spotted a figure standing several yards away to his left. The figure didn't move, and Dusty didn't peg it as an immediate threat. He gave Stafford a long stare. "Dr. Philip Grayson—that's the name of the character you play, isn't it? You're the gent who rescues Connie Smith."

"That's right."

"Well, I think it would be a shame if the noble Dr. Philip Grayson had one eye swollen shut. Might ruin the play for some folks. And, I promise you, the air you're breathing won't seem nearly as nice going through a broken nose. Get inside the church, Stafford."

Charles Stafford glared at the sheriff and laughed in a haughty manner, or tried to, as he turned and walked to the door at the front the church. Barnett gave Phoebe

Martin a kind smile. "Too bad that actor can't be more like the character he plays."

"I guess this was sort of my fault," Phoebe replied in a voice that was little more than a whisper. "I should have been suspicious when Mr. Stafford recommended that we use our break time to go over that scene. But he had been acting more like a gentleman today, and I . . ." She paused, then spoke in a louder, firmer voice. "Mr. Barnett, a lot of people in this town think, well, they think that I'm not a very nice person because I'm in a play. I don't care about most of the gossips, but your opinion does matter to me. I hope that you don't think I'm doing anything wrong."

"Why, I think what you are doing is fine and helpful, Miss Martin." Barnett hoped that his voice was comforting. "Both Brett Connors and Reverend Colt believe that having a play performed here is a good thing for our town. And I feel that way too."

Phoebe gave Dusty an uncertain smile. "What about your deputy? Has he gotten the pebble out of his shoe—I mean, about the play and all?"

Awkward as the question was, Barnett was pleased to hear it. "I think so, Miss Martin. Caleb has a stubborn streak—we both know that—but just give him a little more time. . . ."

"Is everything all right?" Victor Lamont was walking hastily as he came upon the sheriff and the new "Connie Smith." "Stafford is mad as a hornet, yapping to me about how the law in this town is nothing but a bunch of hard cases. I figured that Stafford got out of hand and—"

"Mr. Lamont, I don't think you should allow Charles Stafford to be alone with Miss Martin." Barnett's voice was polite but firm. "Keep an eye on that jasper. There are plenty of folks about who'd love to see me run this theatrical company out of town. Don't hand them any ammunition."

"Of course, Sheriff. You're absolutely right." Victor Lamont paused and looked directly at Phoebe. "I am sorry. It's bad enough that you have to put up with that loathsome newspaperman."

"Has Bradley Stevens been causing trouble?" Barnett asked quickly.

Victor Lamont exchanged grimaces with Phoebe Martin, then answered the question. "Mr. Stevens isn't here right now, but he will probably show up soon. Stevens attends all of our rehearsals, making assurances that he will bring us great fame. The weasel always sits beside Miss Martin or my wife. It's not that he tries to pull anything. . . ."

"Bradley Stevens believes that Jessica and I will soon be groveling at his feet," Phoebe said. "After all, he is going to make us famous actresses, with all of the influence he has in Philadelphia. At first I was impressed by Mr. Stevens—I mean, his being a journalist and all, but—"

"Newspapermen!" Lamont seemed to spit the word from his mouth. "They're worse than actors! Carrying on about how important they are, demanding your time, and, believe me, more often than not, the great article that is going to bring in tremendous crowds ends up being a few lines in the back of the paper or it doesn't get printed at all. I avoid that bunch as much as I can."

Victor Lamont rolled his eyes and shook his head. "I apologize for the outburst. Thank you for your help, Sheriff. I promise to keep Stafford fenced in. Miss Martin, if you're ready, we do need to go over that scene you have with Jessica in the garden. Maybe we'll be lucky, and Bradley Stevens will find some other people to bother tonight."

"Of course, Mr. Lamont." She paused and turned to her other companion. "I appreciate your help, Mr. Barnett, and I certainly hope that you'll enjoy the play tomorrow."

Dusty moved two fingers to his hat. "I'm looking forward to it, Miss Martin."

As the sheriff watched Phoebe walk off beside Victor Lamont, his eyes again glanced to his left as they had done several times since he first spotted the figure standing there. Bert Lassiter almost looked like a military man, standing at attention with his eyes forward, but the slouch in his stance spoiled that illusion.

Barnett felt increasingly strange as he walked toward the actor. Most people, caught staring at someone, would at least look away and pretend to be doing something else besides eavesdropping. Not Bert Lassiter. His eyes remained fixed on the approaching lawman.

"Good evening, Mr. Lassiter."

"Hello, Sheriff."

Barnett didn't know what to say to the actor. After all, standing and staring at other people was not against the law. "Uh, shouldn't you be inside the church rehearsing?"

"They don't need me right now. I'll go inside in a bit."

Dusty was beginning to feel foolish. He decided to ask a pragmatic question. "What do you know about Charles Stafford?"

"Who?"

"Charles Stafford—the man who plays Dr. Grayson. The man who was just bothering Phoebe Martin—" Barnett stopped abruptly. He was going to say, *while you just stood around and did nothing,* but the lawman realized that approach wouldn't help him get any information out of Bert Lassiter.

"Oh. Stafford is a pretty good actor. We've had better Philip Graysons, but he isn't bad."

"What do you know about Stafford personally?"

"Not a thing." Bert Lassiter's face remained completely expressionless as he spoke. "And I don't care. Why should I? You've just seen the way he behaves. Those types never stay long. He'll be gone in six weeks or so, and I will be working with a different Philip Grayson. Sheriff, I can't remember the names or even the faces of most of the Philip Graysons and Connie Smiths I have worked with over just the last six months."

A slight smile suddenly creased the actor's face. "But, you know, once the play starts, it doesn't make any difference what their real names are. They become the handsome, noble Dr. Philip Grayson and the beautiful, innocent Connie Smith. For two hours we are in a different world, a much better world than this one."

The smile vanished, and Bert Lassiter's face again became a blank slate. Barnett thought about what the actor had told him. Lassiter was in a different world, all right, a world the lawman knew he could never fully understand.

"Uh, thank you for your time Mr. Lassiter. I'll let you get back to, uh . . . enjoying the evening."

As Barnett turned to leave, he noticed that an encroaching darkness had reduced the sky's red patch to occasional streaks. He felt uneasy and after walking a few yards turned his head to confirm that, yes, Bert Lassiter was staring at him.

Chapter Twelve

Barnett stepped inside the sheriff's office as Brett Connors, Pat Nolan, and Reverend Colt were talking to Caleb Hodge. "I stopped by the Golden Nugget for a drink," Connors told the sheriff. "Isaac told me what the Gavens brothers are planning." He pointed a thumb at the pastor. "I thought Reverend Colt should know. Now you've got three extra men backing you tonight."

"My deputy and I sure thank you." Barnett smiled as he spoke. "It's nice having friends, especially friends who are good shots."

There were smiles all around. Barnett felt guilty for having questioned Amos Martin about Brett Connors. But he had only been doing his duty. After all, it was not unheard of for a businessman to kill an employee who came across incriminating information.

"Dusty, do the Gavens brothers know that a U.S. Marshal is picking up Cole Hayes tomorrow and taking him to Tucson to stand trial?" Reverend Colt asked.

"They didn't when I talked to them, but they probably do now. It's common knowledge."

"That means they have to make their move tonight," Hodge said.

Brett Connors pointed at the sheriff and his deputy. "We can keep an eye on things here. Why don't you two go over to the Golden Nugget and run those worthless Gavens brothers out of town?"

Barnett shook his head. "That would only stir things up more. We've got to face this head-on. Besides, only two days ago I ordered Earl Beasely and some other barflies to leave Dawson. Can't make that a regular habit."

"What did Beasely do to earn a ticket out of town?" Connors asked.

Barnett caught Caleb Hodge's glance shooting down to the floor. The sheriff shrugged his shoulders in an almost comical manner. "Oh, I guess I was just feeling a bit ornery at the time." Barnett changed the subject. "How is our famous prisoner doing?"

"Our famous prisoner is busy becoming more famous," the deputy answered.

"What—"

Barnett quickly understood what Hodge was saying. Bradley Stevens marched from the jail area into the office. "Sheriff Barnett, I demand that you release Mr. Cole Hayes from that barbaric prison cell immediately! From what I hear, he could soon become the victim of a ruthless gang of vigilantes."

Dusty Barnett moaned out loud before he spoke. "And why should I do that, Mr. Stevens? So that Mr. Cole Hayes, as you call him, can kill more people?"

"Mr. Hayes has killed but only in the defense of widows and orphans," Bradley Stevens declared.

This time Barnett laughed out loud. "What?"

Stevens held up a tablet. "I have the life story of Mr. Cole Hayes right here. He told it to me himself."

Barnett was still laughing. "I'm sure he told you the exact truth."

Brett Connors was more angered than amused. "Mr. Stevens, I think you belong back in Philadelphia."

The journalist gave Connors a haughty look. "I'm not sure that I agree with you, sir."

Barnett stopped laughing. He immediately sensed what Stevens was hinting at. "Are you saying—"

Bradley Stevens' eyebrows arched. "With my next dispatch to the *Philadelphia Tribune,* I may include my resignation. I am thinking about starting a newspaper right here in Dawson."

Brett Connors didn't try to hide his anger. "This town doesn't need someone who—"

"I believe that many of the other businessmen in this town will disagree with you. I am meeting with them within the hour to discuss the possibility of their support through advertising." The look of superiority didn't leave the reporter's face as he turned to Reverend Colt. "Reverend, I can assure you that church news will be featured prominently in my paper. You may want to advise your congregation to pray for the success of this endeavor."

"When word gets around as to what you're up to, Mr. Stevens, I'm sure that many people will feel the need for prayer."

Bradley Stevens looked a bit confused as to how to take the pastor's retort. He settled for a, "Good evening, gentlemen," and, head held high, began a quick exit.

"Mr. Stevens," Barnett called out in a serious tone.

"Yes?" The journalist paused as he opened the door.

"If, after your important meeting, you visit the play rehearsal, behave yourself. You are to leave Phoebe Martin and Jessica Lamont alone."

A look of surprise and anger washed across Stevens' face. He started to say something, then pressed his mouth closed. He settled for looking offended as he marched through the doorway, then slammed the door behind him.

Caleb Hodge glared toward the departed journalist. "Has that dandy been trying to—"

"According to Victor Lamont, he's been more of a pest than anything else." Barnett spoke in a calm voice to his deputy.

"Most of the town thinks he's a pest!" Brett Connors was still angry. "I'd be willing to bet that Stevens won't find a single advertiser for this newspaper that he—"

"You can sure bet that there won't be any advertising from the Golden Nugget," Pat Nolan said.

"There are other problems to worry about, gents,"

Barnett hastily cut in. "To begin with, in a couple of hours, a mob is going to be right outside this office, demanding that we turn over a prisoner." That statement cooled the anger over Bradley Stevens. Barnett continued. "Think I'll have a chat with our 'defender of widows and orphans.' "

"Mind if I come along, Dusty?" Reverend Colt asked. "I'd like to see Cole Hayes in my capacity as a volunteer deputy. Earlier, I tried to visit him as pastor of the Dawson Community Church. I brought him a Bible and offered to talk."

"How did that go?"

"Let's just say that Mr. Hayes' response was brief and not spiritually uplifting."

The jail area contained three cells. Two were empty. Barnett and the clergyman stopped in front of the cell of the infamous gunslick.

"You can't say that this town doesn't appreciate you, Cole." Reverend Colt looked inside Hayes' cell and viewed the dark, empty eyes of the prisoner. "Dawson has provided you with your own private accommodations."

The gunfighter sat on the cot in his cell. He stared at the smoke coming from his cigarette and said nothing.

"Hayes, I'm going to tell it to you plain, which is more than you have ever done for anyone else." Barnett's voice was low, and he couldn't keep the anger out of it. "You probably already know this, but a group of barflies plans to hang you tonight. We're going to stop them."

Cole Hayes turned his head and looked directly at a man he hated. "The mob may be bigger than you think, Sheriff, once that crazy easterner goes 'round tellin' folks how the newspaper in Philadelphia will be sayin' that I only used my gun to protect the weak. Yeah, I think that'll make some people in this town mighty angry."

"Your plan is a smart one, Cole, but it's not going to work." Dusty hoped that he was right.

"What plan is that?" Reverend Colt asked.

As he answered the pastor's question, Barnett stared directly at his prisoner. "Cole is acquainted with the U.S. Marshal who will be here tomorrow morning to take him back to Tucson. They've met before. I also know the marshal. Hayes doesn't have a chance of escaping from that lawman. But if a gang of drunken barflies manages to get him out of this office, well, the odds aren't too bad that Hayes could break away from those jaspers before they get him strung up."

Cole Hayes glared angrily at his captors. "If you think I'm such a low-down snake, Barnett, why not let the mob have me? That pulpit-pounder friend of yours could come along and read words over me. Make it all official and pretty like."

"The west is civilized now, Mr. Hayes," Reverend Colt proclaimed. "We're going to give you a fair trial, *then* we're going to hang you!"

Barnett turned his head and walked away as he stifled a laugh. Reverend Colt trailed behind him, and the two men stopped in front of the closed door that led to the office.

"I apologize for that last remark," the clergyman whispered. He looked both amused and a touch embarrassed. "I guess the humor was in bad taste."

Barnett smiled and shook his head to indicate that nothing was wrong. "Even a pastor is entitled to make a joke now and again."

"I guess so," Reverend Colt replied. "After all, Jesus used humor."

"He did?"

The pastor's expression turned playful. "Remember that verse where Jesus refers to Peter as the rock on which he will build his church?"

"Yes."

"In Greek, *Peter* is *Petros,* and the word for *rock* is *petra.* Jesus was using a bit of wordplay to make his point."

"Oh." Barnett laughed softly.

Reverend Colt made an elaborate shrug. "Okay, so maybe it wasn't exactly a knee-slapper, but the humor was appropriate to the situation."

"Of course."

"We only have a fraction of the words Jesus spoke," the pastor continued. "I'm sure he made remarks that were a lot funnier."

"I don't doubt it." Barnett had never before been involved in a conversation involving words written in the

Greek language. He was genuinely fascinated and wanted to continue, but, as he had said earlier, there was the matter of stopping a lynch mob. He opened the door, and the two men returned to the office.

Brett Connors also returned to the office. He had been standing outside on the boardwalk. "A lot of men are heading for the Golden Nugget. We may be facing a very big mob."

Barnett smiled kindly at the transplanted easterner. "Brett, you're the only one here who has never been involved in an attempted lynching before. In certain ways we're lucky; the situation we're facing tonight could be far worse."

"What do you mean?"

"Sometimes, the so-called good people of a town can all go crazy at the same time—store owners, ranchers, miners, and the like all turn bloodthirsty and demand that a prisoner be turned over to them so they can be judge, jury, and executioner. When that happens, a lawman sometimes has to fire on hardworking people who have never broken a law before in their lives. From what I'm told, it is even worse when a lynch mob succeeds. The people responsible are murderers, and they know it. They are never the same again."

"We don't have that problem tonight," Caleb Hodge said. "This is a more common lynch mob: a bunch of saddle tramps and barflies—the usual troublemakers."

Reverend Colt shook his head in a resigned manner. "Men whose lives don't amount to anything and who think they can change all that by being part of a gang that kills a famous criminal."

Barnett looked directly at Brett Connors, the only man there who needed instruction. "When those jaspers get here, Pat Nolan will cover the back. The rest of us will go outside the office and spread out on the boardwalk. If anyone from the mob tries to step onto the boardwalk, he will be punched a few times as an example to the others. These men are fools, but I don't want to have to kill a man because he is a fool."

"Your help is appreciated, Brett." Reverend Colt gestured toward the sheriff and his deputy. "This is one of the hardest jobs a lawman has—protecting civilization from folks who call themselves civilized."

More than an hour passed before they heard the mob moving toward the sheriff's office. The men stepped outside. After some talk, they had decided that only one of them—Pat Nolan, who was guarding the back—would carry a rifle. They watched as a parade of thugs marched from the Golden Nugget, firing guns, shouting curses, and scorching the air with coarse laughter.

"I'd say there's about twenty of them." Caleb Hodge spoke in a monotone to his boss. "Three on horseback. One of the mounted owl-hoots is leading a riderless horse. Guess that's for Cole Hayes."

The mob was moving quickly, and Barnett had to raise his voice to be heard. "At least they're carrying lanterns, not torches; that's good for Leonard Behan."

A slight look of confusion crossed the deputy's face. Barnett pointed to Behan's Gun Shop across the road. The interior of the store was dark. The owner did not live there. "Drunks carrying lighted torches almost always means fire. I think Len's store will be safe tonight." Even under the circumstances, Barnett had to smile to himself. His interest in the gun shop was a lot more personal than he was ready to admit out loud.

As they had planned, the four men placed some distance between themselves. Caleb Hodge was on one side of Barnett, Brett Connors on the other. The sheriff quickly glanced over Hodge's flat-brimmed hat to look at Reverend Colt. He wasn't concerned about the pastor, who had proven himself before in situations like this one. Barnett couldn't be as sure about Connors. Brett was a good shot but couldn't always control his overly emotional temperament.

The three horsemen rode up to the boardwalk, fired their pistols toward the sky, then circled back toward the gun shop as the throng gathered in front of the sheriff's office. Barnett stared intently at the motley collection of riffraff in front of him. Most of the jaspers would not meet his eyes—a good sign. But this situation was still highly dangerous. One yell could inflame a fight that could leave several men dead.

Blaine and Jeb Gavens both stood close to the boardwalk. Blaine was the first to speak. "Evenin', Sheriff. Lovely night, ain't it?"

The crowd erupted into raucous laughter. Barnett

stood expressionless for a moment before replying. "It's a beautiful night, and I reckon it will be a nice morning. Why don't you gents just move along? That way we can be sure that everyone gets to see the sun come up."

Jeb Gavens angrily pointed a finger at the lawman. "We're here to do justice. We don't need no marshal to take Cole Hayes to Tucson. We can—"

Two shots were fired from above. The four men on the boardwalk and each man in the lynch mob all looked up at the roof of Behan's Gun Shop. "Looks like we're getting a look at the real phantom killer," Barnett said to his deputy.

The figure on the roof was dressed exactly as Phoebe Martin had described Harold Benson's murderer: a black costume like that worn by the menace in the play, only the cape was smaller, and a red bandanna covered his face. And now the predator was holding a pistol in each hand.

"I will decide who lives and dies!" the dark figure shouted, and then he fired a shot in the direction of Brett Connors.

Connors tripped as he darted away from the bullet. Dusty Barnett yelled, "No!" as he realized what Brett was about to attempt. The warning came too late. Falling to the boardwalk, Connors yanked his .45 from its holster and tried to squeeze off a shot. But Connors plunged fast and fired a bullet that ripped into Jeb Gavens, who yelled in pain, staggered, and then dropped to the ground.

"That snake killed my brother! Get him!" Blaine Gavens shouted.

For a brief moment all eyes returned to the rooftop. The phantom killer had vanished. Angry, confused, and frightened, the mob needed an easy target, and Brett Connors provided it. More than a dozen men began to stampede onto the boardwalk as the rest of the mob yelled obscenities at the lawmen.

The horse that was to have carried Cole Hayes to his death reared onto its hind legs, kicked into the air, and galloped off as the barfly who had held the reins let go. One of the three horsemen rode off, either pursuing the horse or getting out of town while it was easy to do. The other two dismounted and joined what was now a riot in front of the sheriff's office.

Connors was back on his feet, his face red. "You're cowards, all of you—nothing but a bunch of worthless jaspers!"

Barnett wanted to take down the leader first. Two hard punches to the head staggered Blaine Gavens. Dusty then hurled Gavens against the front of the sheriff's office. Gavens collided with the wood, sank to the boardwalk, and began to moan loudly. The sheriff hoped that those moans would discourage the rest of the mob.

Caleb Hodge moved directly in front of Connors, whose loud shout had only provoked the crowd. A fist slammed into the deputy's left eye. He responded by punching the offending barfly in the stomach and pushing him against one of his buddies. Both men fell off the boardwalk and showed little interest in mounting another charge.

Connors' anger was ferocious. The one jasper who reached him was knocked to the ground with a fury of punches and then assaulted with several hard kicks.

"That's enough, Brett!" Hodge placed a restraining hand on Connors' chest, then turned to the scuffling sounds behind him. Dusty Barnett had just knocked a hard case onto the ground. Two other men were on the boardwalk, deciding whether to attack Connors.

"I think we should return this gent to his friends." The deputy smiled at Connors and was relieved to see the anger diminish in the businessman's face. Together they picked up the man Connors had beaten and tossed him at the two would-be attackers. Connors' victim screeched in pain as he hit the boards in front of the two men who had jumped back. That settled the matter. They both ran as the jasper who had been airborne began to crawl away.

Reverend Colt used his fists as clubs. He smashed one man in the eye and two others in the nose, causing all three to retreat. He then whipped his gun from its holster and fired over the crowd. "Stop, all of you! Jeb Gavens isn't dead, but he needs help!"

Barnett smiled inwardly at the pastor's move. None of the riffraff gathered in front of the office cared a hoot about Jeb Gavens. But Reverend Colt had given them an excuse to stop fighting. An excuse that most of them, at this point, were looking for.

"Jeb's been shot in the shoulder." The pastor spoke as

he crouched over the younger Gavens and tore away part of his shirt. "We'll put a temporary bandage on the wound, then get him to Doc Jamieson. I'm going to need some help."

The sheriff and his deputy along with Brett Connors watched silently as several members of the mob began to assist Reverend Colt. The other jaspers quickly walked away or, in more than a few cases, staggered away.

"There is just one little chore left to this evening's work." Barnett smiled at his companions, then walked over to Blaine Gavens, who was still lying in front of the office. Gavens' hands were cupped around his head as he continued to emit groans of pain.

Barnett spoke in a loud, mockingly friendly voice. "Blaine, I have good news for you. You're so interested in the famous Cole Hayes that I'm going to put you into a cell right beside him. Why, Mr. Bradley Stevens might even mention your name in one of the articles he writes about how Cole does so much for the widows and orphans. You'll be well known all over Philadelphia."

Blaine Gavens added a streak of curses to his groans.

"The gent seems to have lost his sense of humor," Barnett observed.

The sheriff took one last look around him as he stood on the roof of Behan's Gun Shop. He couldn't spot anything that would help identify the owl-hoot who had been on the roof over an hour before wearing the phantom killer outfit and firing a gun. The lawman sighed as he admitted to himself that he didn't exactly know what he was looking for.

Dusty Barnett climbed back onto a rickety ladder that was propped against the back of the gun shop and cautiously made his way downward, where Caleb Hodge and Brett Connors were waiting for him.

"Afraid I didn't find anything," the sheriff said as he stepped off the bottom rung.

Brett Connors was paying more attention to the ladder than he was to the lawman. "What a stupid thing to do! I left that fool thing lying behind the stage depot. But I've been doing some work on the roof there, and the ladder is in such bad condition, I never thought anyone—"

"Forget it, Brett," Barnett cut in. "Our phantom friend would have found some way to get up there even without your ladder."

"I can't help but feel that the killer was sending some kind of message." Connors' voice was heavy with tension.

"What do you mean?" Barnett asked.

"Last Tuesday night, Harold Benson, a man who has been prominent with the stagecoach line since it came to Dawson, was murdered while he was working in the stage depot. Tonight, the killer stole a ladder from the depot, climbed up onto the roof of Behan's Gun Shop, and took a shot at me, the man whose family owns the stage line and the man who is in charge of the company here in Dawson, or is supposed to be."

"It does sound like it's all connected," Caleb Hodge said. "You got any idea who may be after you, Brett?"

"None."

"Whoever it was didn't use a horse." Barnett once again examined the ground behind the store.

"He must have been mighty confident that he could get away." Hodge pushed his hat back and scratched his head as if trying to hurry along the thinking process. "I mean, what if the killer had been successful tonight? Sure, one of us would have stayed with Brett, but he had to have figured that someone would come after him."

"Yeah, you'd think so," Barnett replied. "The way I see it, our spook got up onto the roof, made his little speech, fired at Brett, then dropped down where no one could see him to return fire. Wouldn't have been hard for him to crawl back to where the ladder was and run off while that riot was going on."

"A riot I caused by shooting Jeb Gavens." Connors again berated himself. "At least the wound wasn't too serious."

"Maybe our phantom sort of counted on something like that," Barnett speculated. "With a crowd of liquored-up barflies, starting a riot wouldn't have been that hard."

"One thing's for sure, one of my hopes about all this is gone," Caleb Hodge said.

Both of his companions looked quizzically at the deputy. He straightened his hat as he spoke. "Guess I had sort of a hope that the killer was someone from the outside who'd ridden into town and then left. But, no, the phantom killer didn't use a horse tonight. He just took off his costume and started going about his business normal like."

Caleb Hodge sighed deeply, then continued. "Whoever did this is no stranger. It's someone who is living right here among us."

Chapter Thirteen

Fred Bostick closed the dime novel and placed it on the crudely constructed table where he did paperwork for the livery stable. He stood up and looked over the three rows of stalls and their occupants.

"Guess it must be past midnight, fellas and gals. I should be turnin' in soon." Fred had long ago lost any inhibitions about talking to the horses; he even did it when other people were around. "But after all that commotion at the sheriff's office tonight, I thought it smart to sit up a spell. One of those troublemakers might decide to leave town quick and, bein' in a hurry and all, might interrupt your evenin' repose without payin' me for your hard work."

Fred Bostick laughed at his own joke—another inhibition he had long ago discarded. With the instinct of a well-trained animal, the livery owner began his prebedtime routine. He walked around the stable, examining each animal and giving it a friendly pat. He then took a lantern and walked out through the back doors.

Behind the stable was a corral that tonight held seven horses. The animals all seemed content. There were four buckboards of various sizes lined up between the right side of the stable and the corral. Bostick's Blacksmith and Livery owned five buckboards. One had been rented out. A mound of hay was piled against the back wall of the building on the left side.

As he did every night, Fred Bostick circled his property twice. His mind drifted to the excitement at the sheriff's office earlier that evening, and he wished that he had been there. Seeing the phantom killer in person, firing his guns from the roof of a building—yes, by golly, that would have been something.

Fred reentered the stable by the front doors, then placed the long, thick wooden bar across the holders in the two doors. "That should do it." A few of his companions neighed in response. He repeated the procedure with the back doors, then climbed up a stack of crates and closed the shutters on the stable's window.

One of the horses snorted as he climbed down. "Yeah, yeah, I know. One shutter is about to fall off, and that's little more than a stick holdin' 'em shut. I'll git around to it soon enough."

The horse responded with more steam shooting from its nose.

"I would do it now, but my bad arm aches." Fred's voice took on a plaintive tone. "Some folks 'round here say that when they get an ache, it means the weather's 'bout to change. Not me. I ain't no prophet, jus' an old man with a bum arm."

Fred Bostick and his son, Ryan, were joint owners of Bostick's Blacksmith and Livery. Fred had started the business seventeen years back and had quickly gained a reputation as being one of the best blacksmiths in the Arizona Territory. He had managed to keep that reputation even after an ornery horse landed a hard kick to his left arm, permanently injuring it. But, these days, Fred mostly took care of the livery end of the business and left the blacksmith chores to his son.

Fred chuckled to himself as he carried the lantern back to the table. Ryan thought his old man was a saint for staying at the stable every night and allowing him to be at their house with his wife and three kids. Well, let him keep thinking that. Fred loved his grandkids but chose to love them from a distance. On most nights he preferred the company of horses and dime-novel heroes.

He placed the kerosene lantern on the table and picked up the book he had just completed: *Buffalo Bill: His Adventures in the West,* by Ned Buntline. The cover featured Buffalo Bill lying on top of a passenger car of a fast-moving train, firing his rifle at a gang of owl-hoots. The cover showed the trajectory of Bill's shot as it entered the chest of one of the outlaws.

Fred wondered how much of the story was based on fact and then decided that he really didn't care. He smiled at his friends. "That Buntline can shore write a good yarn."

One of the horses turned her head and stared at him directly. Fred stared back in a slightly nervous manner. "I know a man's supposed to read the Good Book, and I do!" He picked up a black-covered tome from a corner of the table and waved it at the nag. "Read it every night, but there's nothin' wrong with readin' other stuff too."

The horse turned its head away and snorted. Fred placed the book back on the table, not certain whether or not he had won the argument. The hostler decided not to worry about it anymore. He put out the lantern, lay down on a bed of blankets and straw, and went to sleep.

Fred Bostick awoke to the sounds of nervous nickering. He lay still and listened. Cautious footsteps could be heard in the stable. In a mechanical, efficient manner, Fred lit a kerosene lantern and grabbed a Peacemaker, both of which he kept close to his bed.

The light revealed that the shutters had been opened on the window of the livery. He could hear the intruder but not see him. The man was on the other side of the stalls, either crawling or waddling like a duck.

Fred sprung up quickly from his bed, the lantern in one hand and the gun in the other. "Okay, friend, I'm givin' ya one chance to do this polite like. Hold up your hands, and let me see who you are." Bostick was quiet for a moment; so was the unwanted guest. "Maybe you've seen me in town and think the livery is easy pickin's. Well, you're plumb wrong. Anyone in Dawson will tell ya that Fred Bostick is a good shot, bad arm and all. Show yourself right now. I ain't askin' again!'"

Bostick spotted a hand reaching up from the ground, grabbing the bar that was across the back doors and pushing it off. The doors were shoved open. Fred Bostick ran across the livery, between two rows of stalls, and didn't let up on speed as he dashed through the back exit.

Outside, Fred stopped and became more cautious. His eyes went immediately to the corral. All of the horses were there. He moved the lantern around, looking for signs of the intruder. The light fell on one of the back doors, and the hostler could see shoes in the space between the door and the ground.

"Okay, stranger, don't be stupid." Bostick pointed his Peacemaker toward the door. "So far you ain't done nothin' too bad. Jus' step out, and we'll take us a walk to the sheriff's office."

A harsh, mocking laugh cut the air. A figure dressed in black with a red mask, who only hours before had been on top of the gun shop, now stepped from behind the door. "No jail can hold the phantom killer." The phantom swaggered toward Fred Bostick. "I would like to see you try to march me to the sheriff's office." This time the phantom killer's laugh was softer but no less threatening. "Go ahead! I'm not armed." The mysterious figure stopped and pushed back his cape, revealing that there were no guns strapped to his waist. "By all means, let us begin our little walk together."

Fred Bostick took two steps backward. He dropped the lantern, which didn't break but now cast a more skewered light on the phantom killer; half of him could be seen, but the other half was shrouded by darkness. Fred looked down and saw that the Peacemaker was shaking in his hand.

Bostick took a deep breath and felt ashamed of himself. His hand steadied, and the terror that had run through him subsided. "I ain't scared of no fool play-actor's outfit!"

The costumed figure nodded toward the ground. "Really? I suppose a little bird knocked that lantern right out of your hand."

"Okay, you spooked me some at first—I admit it—but no longer." Fred lifted the Peacemaker a bit higher and, using his bad arm, set the lantern upright on the ground. "The show's over. Take off that mask."

The phantom killer placed both hands on his hips. "You've got the gun. Why don't you rip the mask off?"

"Jus' maybe I will."

The phantom killer became a blur as Fred Bostick's head flopped about beyond his control. The hostler staggered and tried to keep his balance as pain and dizziness ravaged him. That terrible laugh sounded once again. "You have learned a lesson, my friend. Never oppose the phantom killer."

"I still have a gun. You'd better . . ." Fred tried to raise his weapon, but the Peacemaker slipped from his hand. The ground moved up and slammed him in the face.

Chapter Fourteen

Cool morning air used to invigorate Caleb Hodge but no longer. His mind was too fixed on how mornings once were, not very long ago. After his first round was over, customarily he would stop at Martin's Restaurant, and he and Phoebe would have breakfast together. He didn't know how the girl felt about it, but for him it was the best part of the day.

Hodge walked around the Fast Horse Saloon. He rousted three saddle tramps who were sleeping off the previous night's revelry. The deputy managed to wake the men and get them to sit up but didn't have the time to wait until they got onto their feet. "I'll be back soon, and you gents had better be gone."

"Yeah, yeah, sure . . ." All three jaspers mumbled curses as each one placed a hand over his head and generally appeared miserable. "Some folks just never learn," Hodge muttered to himself, and he continued on his round.

The deputy's amusement over the saddle tramps quickly vanished as his thoughts returned to Phoebe Martin. Of course, the woman had a polite explanation for why she could no longer have breakfast with him. There just wasn't time. Her father was busy helping Brett Connors, and she had to rehearse for the play. Why, with all that going on, she just couldn't plan ahead for when she'd be able to have breakfast.

Women are good at that, he thought, *thinking up polite and nice reasons for acting plumb loco.* "Guess I haven't helped matters much," Hodge said aloud to himself as he walked toward Bostick's Blacksmith and Livery. When Phoebe had told him it was true that she was acting in a play, he had declared, "A woman who play-acts is just like a woman who works in a saloon. . . ."

The deputy stopped for a moment, kicked some dirt, then continued his round. Dusty Barnett had been helping him to control his temper. He supposed that he still had a lot more to learn in that area.

Caleb thought about apologizing to Phoebe and wondered how she would respond. Would she even care? As the deputy approached the left side of the livery, he admitted to himself that Phoebe didn't seem to place much value on his opinion of her being in a play and all, and that bothered him. It bothered him a lot.

Hodge spotted the open window at the side of the livery. Fred shuttered that window every night, and every morning he took the bars off the doors before attending to the window. The doors were still closed. Low moans came from behind the stable, and Caleb ran toward them.

Fred Bostick was leaning against the back wall of the livery in obvious pain. He took a few uncertain steps away from the building as Caleb approached.

"Fred, what happened?"

"Gotta be careful." The hostler's voice wavered in a whirlpool of nausea and dizziness. "Came to during the night and tried to get up. Jus' fell down and made things worse."

With the deputy staying close beside him, Fred Bostick staggered toward the corral. "That goblin stole four of my horses." He carefully turned to where the buckboards were lined up. "Took one of my wagons. The smallest one. Right nice of him to be so thoughtful."

"Who, Fred? Who did this to you?"

"Ya wouldn't believe it if I tol' ya." Fred placed a hand on the corral to steady himself. "Course, crazy as things have been lately, maybe ya would believe it. . . ."

Bostick related the events of that evening as well as he could, pausing to make the occasional joke about the pain in his head being worse than anything he ever got from drinking tanglefoot. Fred's account was accurate and honest, and he didn't skip over his initial fear at the sudden appearance of the man who called himself the phantom killer.

"Appreciate it if ya wouldn't tell nobody 'bout how I let that costumed fool scare me. Don't mind ya tellin' Dusty, he bein' the sheriff and all . . ."

"Don't worry, Fred." Caleb spoke in a kind, cheerful voice. "Besides, that phantom killer needed an accomplice to steal from Bostick's. The way I see it, someone else broke in through the window. He made enough noise to get you to follow him outside, where the phantom was waiting. The accomplice probably hid behind the buckboards and crept up slowly on you while the phantom killer served as a distraction.

"And that no-good jasper had to hit me twice before I went down!" Fred declared proudly. "Both my wife, God rest her soul, and my daughter-in-law say that I'm hardheaded. Guess they got proved right!"

"They sure did. Come on, Fred, we'll walk over to Doc Jamieson's place and get you patched up."

"Thanks," the hostler said. "I could . . . well . . . if that ain't a mule kick!"

"What do you mean?"

Fred pointed toward the barn. "That hill of hay ain't so big anymore. Guess the phantom fella took some of it."

The deputy smirked. "I guess even a phantom needs to feed his horses. As soon as you're at the doctor's place, I'll fetch Ryan. He can take care of the business by himself today. You'll need to go home and get some rest."

"I'll come back here," Fred responded quickly. "No way I'd get any rest with them young'uns all around."

Zack Beal kept a loose rein on the horses—no need to do otherwise. The nags had made this trip to Dawson many times before. In fact, the horses could probably move the stagecoach without him, but Zack wasn't about to tell anyone that.

The midmorning sun was a bit hot but not really too bad. The stagecoach driver was in a good mood. They were less than two miles from Dawson; a soothing bath, a comfortable bed, and a bit of poker at the Fast Horse Saloon awaited him. And, yes, by golly, he would go to the play. He'd never seen anything like that before, and, while he'd never admit it, he was looking forward to seeing *The Phantom Killer.*

"Say, Zack, that one passenger we got, the drummer, what do you suppose he's selling?"

Well, no day can be perfect, Zack thought. Yancey, his shotgun, was a nice boy, but he was a boy. Zack preferred the company of Hawk Pickford, but Hawk was still recovering from the wounds he got in the holdup attempt a few days back.

"Don't know!" the driver shouted back. "I'm not the brightest star in the sky, but I got enough sense not to ask a drummer what he's selling!"

"He's dressed mighty fine. I figure he's selling clothes. I could use some new duds, impress the ladies. . . ."

Zack went back to ignoring his shotgun. He wondered if he had been that thickheaded when he was young. *Probably,* he reckoned.

"Something's wrong up ahead, Zack!"

The driver looked intently but could see nothing.

Still, he stopped ignoring his shotgun and slowed the horses. Yancey's eyes were a lot better than his.

"There's a horse beside the road." Yancey pointed to his left. "And I think there's a man lying on the road."

Zack brought the stagecoach to a stop, glanced briefly at the horse, then at the figure that lay on the ground a few yards from the coach. "Can't tell if it's anyone I know—that Stetson covers his head."

"Need any help?" The shout came from inside the coach.

"Maybe," the driver shouted down to his passenger. "Got a man injured up ahead."

The drummer disembarked from the driver's side of the coach and began to walk very hesitantly toward the injured man. Despite himself, Zack admired the drummer. The salesman was obviously a bit squeamish about the possibility of seeing a crushed skull or similar injury, but he still wanted to be a Good Samaritan.

"His nag probably got spooked by a snake or something and threw him." As he spoke, Yancey placed his rifle on top of the coach and jumped off. He hurried toward the victim, then stopped suddenly and examined the horse that was munching grass beside the road.

"That sure is strange," Yancey said.

"What's strange?" Zack shouted the question. The drummer stopped a comfortable distance from the body lying on the road.

"This horse has been tethered to the ground, real careful like. There's a pile of stones neatly piled up."

"Yancey, a man might be dying." Zack continued to shout. "You can worry about the horse later."

Yancey moved quickly to the body and crouched over it. He gasped, then began to laugh. The drummer's face turned curious, and he took several steps toward the body to get a better view.

"What's so dern funny?" The driver was becoming increasingly irritated with his shotgun.

"This fella is made of hay!" Yancey ripped a glove from the body's hand, scattering hay into the air. "No wonder he tethered his horse so good. If he hadn't, the horse might have eaten him!"

Yancey and the drummer began to laugh. Zack wasn't amused. Anger coursed through him as he realized that he had been fooled. He turned to grab his weapon, but a gunshot made him freeze.

"Leave that rifle where it is, my friend." A figure in a black costume and red mask stepped out from behind a large boulder at the side of the road. He carried a six-gun in each hand.

"Mercy!" The drummer's voice was a high-pitched squeak.

"You're the phantom killer!" Yancey shouted angrily. "Like that man in the playacting, but you're real."

"Very real, my friend." The phantom spoke with a tinge of glee. "And I know that real men can behave dangerously. We will have none of that here. I want you and the well-dressed gentleman to walk around to this side of the coach. Stand beside the horses."

The drummer began to follow instructions, then stopped, obviously confused when he saw that Yancey wasn't moving. The young man was glaring defiantly at the robber.

"Move now! You want to get people killed?" The phantom no longer sounded gleeful. Yancey and the drummer did what they were told.

The phantom pointed one gun directly at Zack. "There are two rifles behind you. Throw each one down carefully and slowly."

As he tossed Yancey's Winchester .44 to the ground, Zack spotted a flash of light from behind the boulder. The sun was reflecting off a gun. This was not a one-man job. The driver threw down his own weapon.

"Very good." The phantom once again sounded cheerful. "Soon our work will be done, and you can be on your way. Now throw down the strongbox."

Zack obeyed. When the strongbox collided with the ground, the phantom whirled and pointed a gun at Yancey, who had taken a step toward him.

"I won't warn you again, my impetuous friend." The phantom's voice remained mockingly friendly but still threatening.

"Stop being a fool!" Perspiration ran down the drummer's face.

"Just do what you're told, Yancey." Zack spoke calmly, hoping that calmness would transfer itself to his young colleague.

A look of resignation came over Yancey's face. He took a step back and stood beside the drummer.

"Excellent." The phantom returned his attention to the driver. "Now toss down that bag."

Zack looked confused as he glanced at his skimpy cargo. "The mailbag?"

"Yes, my friend. People often send valuables through the mail. While you do that, I want you other two gentlemen to step inside the coach."

Everyone did as they were instructed. As Zack tossed down the mailbag, he looked for indications of another gunman hiding behind the rock. He spotted nothing but remained sure that someone was there.

"Out little get-together is over." The phantom spoke as the mailbag hit the ground. "I wish you all a good day. And for your evening's entertainment, I recommend taking in a play. I understand that *The Phantom Killer* is being performed in Dawson tonight!"

The costumed figure fired both pistols into the air. Zack yelled at the horses, and they lurched into a fast gallop, creating a massive dust cloud. Over the pounding hoofbeats, a loud, piercing laugh could be heard.

Dusty Barnett and Caleb Hodge were riding slowly as they followed a trail. The job was too easy, and both men sensed that something was wrong.

"This just don't make sense." Hodge looked up from studying the fresh ruts in the road. "Why would this phantom use a buckboard and four horses to rob the stage? One horse is a lot easier to hide and a lot harder to follow."

"Yeah, but remember, Zack thinks there were two men involved in the holdup."

"So do I," Caleb responded immediately. "The guy hiding behind the boulder was the same one who helped with the robbery at the livery, if you ask me. But, still, why would they need a buckboard? And the robber knew that there were two rifles—"

"Most folks know that both the driver and shotgun have a rifle on board the stagecoach. Nothing—What's this?" Barnett pointed to several pieces of paper that were tumbling across the road a few yards in front of them. Both men dismounted and ran toward four letters that were being battered about by a light wind. The lawmen then followed a wavy line of mail, which led into a grove of trees.

The buckboard that had been stolen from Bostick's Blacksmith and Livery was now standing amid the trees. The four horses were contentedly munching on grass and leaves. Barnett stuffed the letters he had picked up back into the open mailbag, which lay on the seat. Hodge examined the empty strongbox, which had been left beside the wagon.

"They took the money from the strongbox, took everything valuable from the mailbag, then walked back into Dawson!" the deputy shouted angrily. "They're probably having a drink right now and laughing about how they treed us!"

"You said before that this whole thing didn't make much sense." Barnett ignored his deputy's anger. "You were right."

"I don't follow you."

"Think about the drummer," Barnett said.

"What about him?"

"You can't tell with a drummer," Barnett explained. "The man may be carrying a fat wallet or have nothing in his pocket except lint. Still, you saw those swell duds he was wearing. You'd think a robber would make him empty his pockets. What's more, the drummer had a bag on top of the coach. The phantom didn't even ask to see it."

"That is crazy. Of course, the whole town seems to have gone crazy since those playactors arrived."

"Do you mind taking the buckboard back to the Bosticks' place?"

"No."

"Thanks. I'll ride back into town." Barnett paused, then decided to prod his deputy a bit. "After you return the buckboard, there will be some time to stop in the stores, maybe take up that idea I mentioned."

To Barnett's surprise, Caleb Hodge did not become angry. "You really think I should get her a present?" The question was sincere.

"Sure," Dusty replied casually. "Phoebe is being an

actress in the first play ever done in Dawson. I think that deserves a little special recognition."

Caleb Hodge patted one of the horses. "Maybe so."

Riding back into town, Dusty Barnett felt good. Caleb Hodge was growing up fast. Dawson would have a fine man for its next sheriff.

Chapter Fifteen

Dusty Barnett returned to his office, hastily put his hat on a peg, and opened the bottom drawer of his desk, where he had placed the letters that Amos Martin had given him. As he tossed the letters onto the desktop and settled into the chair, he felt uneasy, as if he were doing something low-down.

Barnett thought about the unique friendship Harold Benson had with the Connors family. For fifteen years, Harold had written to Thaddeus Connors and then to Thaddeus' widow, Abigail. Of course, much of that correspondence consisted of information about the stage depot, which the Connors family owned, but it must have gone beyond that. From what Amos had said, it was obvious that a very strong friendship and trust had developed between people who had not seen each other for many years and would never see each other again. Barnett wondered if he ever could have maintained such a friendship.

Maybe that was why he felt so odd about the letters

and had been putting off reading them. He felt as if he was intruding into something fine that didn't concern him. But, of course, it did concern him.

Barnett began to skim through the letters, which, as he had figured, consisted of a mix of personal news and information about the stage depot. But he carefully read one letter written almost a year earlier.

Harold, I write these words with a sense of shame. You and Clara have been like family to us. You helped Louis Connors to live a decent, respectable life there in Dawson, and we are forever in your debt. You should now be rewarded by becoming the manager of the depot. Instead, I am asking you to assume yet another burden for the Connors family.

My nephew, Brett, has become a heartbreak to his parents, both of whom are getting along in years. Brett was the youngest in his family, a beautiful child, and I am afraid he was spoiled. He has become an indolent young man, wasting his life on hedonistic pursuits such as gambling and attending the theater. He enjoys spending time with theater people and regards himself as a patron of the arts. I take that to mean that he buys drinks for the actors and who knows what for the actresses, and they, in turn, put up with him.

Barnett laughed out loud and felt a bit embarrassed. Of course, he could never josh Brett about something in a private letter, though resisting the temptation would be hard. Barnett reckoned that he had to be careful not to reveal that he knew about Brett's private family matters and then read on.

As you know, my dear Thaddeus always regarded the west as a place where a man can become a man and find a new life. I have agreed to pay Brett's gambling debts in exchange for his promise to move to Dawson and become manager of the stage depot.

Abigail went on, at length, to state how unfair this move was, but she was hoping that Harold could help Brett in the same way that he had helped Louis Connors. The rest of the letter assured Harold that he need not be concerned that the family was concentrating most of its business interests in matters outside of the stage line. Even if the railroad did come into Dawson, Abigail was confident that the area would need a stagecoach for at least the immediate future. Harold's position would not be threatened. Barnett became increasingly embarrassed as he read the details of the economic relationship between Harold Benson and the Connors family. Amos Martin was right: Harold's hard work and loyalty had received a just reward. Barnett was also happy to learn that the arrangement included benefits for Harold's widow. Clara Benson would have no money problems.

The letters gradually became more upbeat as Abigail

delighted over the many improvements the west had bestowed upon her wayward nephew. The final letter, the one that had arrived after Harold's murder and was read by Brett Connors and Amos Martin, was the most effusive.

My dear Thaddeus was so right about the wonders of the west! From your letters, I know that my pale, sullen, skinny nephew has become a robust man, friendly to all and responsible in matters of business. Harold, despite your modest claims to the contrary, I know that you and Clara have been an indispensable help to my nephew. You are both wonderful people and an answer to prayer.

Alas, in response to your request, I have no picture of Brett that could be hung in the office. But I am sending along a family picture taken last year, which, of course, includes Brett. I should have the picture in the mail by the end of the week. The Connors family does not have enough pictures like this one! Our family is now very big and, I fear, too busy. We do not spend enough time together. . . .

Barnett hastily read the rest of Abigail's message, then folded the letters back into their envelopes and returned them to his desk drawer.

The sheriff walked over to the front window and looked outside but saw nothing. His mind fastened onto the various small details concerning Harold Benson's murder that made no sense, that just didn't seem to fit anywhere.

Then he began to make vague connections, and a pattern formed. But that pattern was pretty hazy. Dusty Barnett reclaimed his hat from the peg and hurried from the office. He had some questions to ask.

Caleb Hodge appeared nervous as he walked into the sheriff's office. "Afternoon."

"Afternoon." Barnett remained at his desk, looking over circulars.

"Took your advice." The deputy began to check the rifles in the rack on the office wall.

"Oh?"

"Stopped at Ellie Poston's store."

Barnett had to suppress a laugh; just walking through the door of that place must have been agony for Caleb. "That's good. Mrs. Poston sells some very pretty things."

"Yeah, didn't know what a lot of that stuff was."

"I'm sure you picked out something nice that Miss Martin will deeply appreciate."

"Hope so."

Caleb was becoming increasingly nervous, and Barnett was glad that he had official business to discuss. "You're going to have to miss the first few minutes of the play."

"Why's that?"

Barnett dropped the circulars onto a corner of the desk and informed his deputy about the letters from Abigail Connors to Harold Benson. The sheriff concluded by noting, "I figure that about fifteen minutes before curtain time, as the theater people call it, practically the whole town will be gathering in front of the church."

"Probably so."

"Reverend Colt and Pat Nolan will be there to keep an eye on things. You and I will be breaking into a man's house."

"What?"

Dusty got up and leaned against the desk. "Many years ago, I learned a lot about being a lawman from a thief named Dog Bark. Bark was his real last name—guess he got tagged 'Dog' when he was a kid."

"What did this Dog teach you?"

"Dog was different." Barnett smiled as he spoke; the memory was pleasant for him. "He never robbed banks or anything like that. He would take a job as a hand on a large ranch, watch the family that owned the ranch carefully, then one day break into the ranch house and steal jewelry and other valuables."

"How did he get into the safe?"

"He didn't." Barnett's smile widened. "Dog told me that people would always keep valuables that they used often—like jewelry, watches, and such—in the bedroom. Since that is the most private room in the house, people tend to think it's also the safest. Of course, it was the first room Dog would visit. But it was something that Dog told me about the way men behave that I remember the most."

"What might that be?"

"Dog said that a man living alone will always hide something shameful in his bedroom—even if he has a safe. That safe contains important papers from his respectable life, and he doesn't want to mix the two. Besides, there could be business partners with him when he opens the safe."

Caleb Hodge looked thoughtful. "Makes sense, kind of. Sounds like Dog was talking from experience."

Barnett nodded. "Dog once broke into a rancher's bedroom to steal a valuable watch. The rancher owned half of a worthless mine in California. Dog found some letters from a friend of the rancher in San Francisco, who owned the other half of the worthless property. They were planning to salt the mine and sell it to some gullible easterners. Dog would have had to work a year to earn what the rancher paid him to get those letters back."

"Dog sure knew how to profit from an hour or so of work," Hodge said. "But what does all this have to do with us missing part of the play?"

"Tonight, while the whole town is at the church, we're visiting the bedroom of Brett Connors."

Brett Connors' bedroom was large and looked lived in. A desk was fronted by scratch marks and indentations on the floor where the chair had been frequently moved about. This was where Brett handled his personal correspondence, not the desk in the sitting room, which appeared ornate but untouched. Barnett lit a kerosene lamp that stood on a bedside table and pointed toward a chest of drawers. "You start there. I'll take the closet."

"Wish I knew what I was looking for." Nervousness wavered through Hodge's voice.

"Remember what Dog—"

"Yeah, yeah, something shameful," the deputy replied.

The mention of Dog Bark caused the sheriff to reflect on where the thief had found those letters about the salted mine. For a moment he forgot about the closet and lifted the mattress on the bed. "Dog sure understood human nature." Barnett pulled out a large brown envelope, then gently lowered the mattress back into position and placed his find on top of it.

"What do you have there?" Hodge walked over carrying a piece of paper he had found in the top drawer of the chest.

"The envelope has been opened. Let's find out." Barnett pulled out two pieces of stiff cardboard. Between them was a large family portrait. "There must be close to thirty people in this picture." As Barnett spoke, he noticed names on one of the pieces of cardboard. "This is the family portrait that Abigail Connors wrote Harold about. She has the names of everyone charted here. According to Abigail, Brett Connors is standing in the top row, third from left."

Caleb Hodge stared at the photo carefully. "Sure doesn't look much like Brett to me. Of course, he's shaved that mustache since the picture got took."

"Maybe."

"Brett doesn't have a mustache now, so he must—"

"You know what made me suspicious about Brett Connors to start with?" Barnett interrupted.

"No."

"A conversation I had with Victor Lamont." Barnett answered his own question, then explained how the previous night he had been doing a round when he caught Charles Stafford getting carried away while rehearsing a scene with Phoebe. "After Stafford went back into the church, Lamont came out and apologized to Miss Martin. He also told me that Bradley Stevens had made quite a nuisance of himself. Seems that Mr. Victor Lamont doesn't care much for reporters. I didn't think on it much at the time—had other things on my mind. We had to keep Cole Hayes safe until the U.S. Marshal arrived."

Hodge shrugged. "What was there to think on?"

"A few days back, Bradley Stevens told us that Lamont had sent letters out to a lot of eastern newspapers, telling them that his troupe was to perform in a hick town where most of the rubes had never seen a play."

A look of excitement ignited in the deputy's face. "Doesn't sound like something a man who doesn't like reporters would do."

"I asked Lamont about it this afternoon," Barnett

continued. "He denied sending those letters. I checked with the telegraph office. Percy told me that Brett Connors had asked him to let him know if a Victor Lamont received any telegrams. Connors claimed that Lamont was traveling about but would be in town soon and had asked him to take care of his messages. Made sense to Percy. Besides, Lamont only received one telegram."

"Brett Connors sent out those letters!" Hodge spoke excitedly. "And he only got one fish from his bait: Bradley Stevens."

"And Stevens wired when he was coming. Brett hired three saddle tramps to rob the stage. But the plan backfired, and the robbers were almost captured. I thought Brett was reacting to his first gunfight when he killed those two men. I was wrong. He was killing men who could implicate him in the holdup."

"But why would Brett hold up his own stagecoach?"

Dusty Barnett looked down at the picture and then glanced at the large shadows the lamp cast upon the walls. "Brett wanted the eastern papers filled with stories about what a wide-open, lawless town Dawson is—stagecoaches getting robbed, a weird character in a play jumping off the stage and committing a real murder. . . ."

"But why?"

"So the railroad folks would decide to stay away from Dawson. That would mean a lot more money for the stagecoach line."

"Doesn't make sense, Dusty. If the railroad came, this area would still need a stagecoach, at least for a while.

The Connors family is rich—they're into all sorts of businesses. Even if the stagecoach did fold, they could find Brett—"

Barnett's shadow stretched out as he walked away from the bed and began to pace the room. "The man who calls himself Brett Connors is an imposter. The real Brett Connors is dead."

"What!"

Barnett stopped pacing and faced his deputy. "Abigail wrote Harold that her nephew was a man who liked to hang out with theater folks. On his way to Dawson, Brett Connors probably had a stopover for a few days in Denver. Not hard to imagine that he would take in a play, then hang out with the actors. While he was buying one of the actors some drinks, Brett blubbered about having to move to Dawson to manage the stage line. That actor saw an opportunity for big money. He killed Brett Connors, stole his identification, and took his hotel key. He then went to the hotel, carefully went over the room of Brett Connors, and he became Brett Connors."

Caleb Hodge waved the paper he had in his hand. "This letter I found in the chest of drawers backs up what you're saying." Hodge began to read: " 'Dearest Mother and Father, I am spending three days in Denver. Three more days in civilization before I have to carry out this insane scheme of my crazy aunt. Don't worry, I will keep my promise about the gambling. I plan to see a production of *No Time For Romance* tonight. Will write more later.' "

Barnett peered for a moment over his deputy's shoulder. "Connors wrote his parents' address at the top. And the man we call Brett Connors kept that letter, so he could imitate the handwriting for the letters he later sent to the parents of Brett Connors."

"But why would he keep the picture?"

"In case one of the relatives came out west to check up on things in Dawson. The people who knew Brett really well are too old now to make the trip. Abigail complained in one of her letters that the family didn't see much of each other. So, the man we have been calling Brett Connors studies that photo regularly. If, one day, a cousin walks into the office, Brett can greet him by name. The cousin hasn't seen Brett for a few years. The mustache is gone. I think it would work."

"Guess this phony Connors felt that he had to get that picture before it got to the office." Hodge spoke softly, thinking out loud. "Amos Martin is handling all the mail for now. It would have looked pretty suspicious for him to tell Amos not to open a package from the Connors family."

"Right."

Caleb Hodge pushed back his hat and scratched his head. "This fellow who is passing himself off as Brett Connors must be a pretty good actor. He sure has everyone fooled."

"He didn't fool Harold Benson. Harold wrote to Abigail asking for a picture of Brett to hang on the wall of the office, or so he claimed. If you ask me, Harold was suspicious of his new boss."

"That suspicion cost him his life." Caleb looked down at the floor and shook his head.

"Harold's life had been in danger since the phony Brett Connors arrived. With Harold around, Connors had to stay honest. The man we call Connors brought the acting troupe to town and managed to get one eastern reporter here. He planned to get rid of Harold and the railroad with one killing. This jasper who is posing as Connors is an actor, so he knows all about *The Phantom Killer* play. Making a costume wouldn't be tough."

"But this phantom killer was on the roof of Behan's Gun Shop last night while Brett was standing across the street."

Barnett nodded. "The man we call Brett Connors has someone helping him."

"Who?"

"I have an idea but can't prove anything." Barnett took the letter from his deputy. "I'll finish searching in here. You've got a play to attend."

"But—"

"I'll be along soon." Barnett waved him away.

"If I see Connors—"

"Brett Connors will be no threat to anyone tonight. He's playing the role of, well, Brett Connors, good citizen and patron of the arts."

"Yeah, guess so." Hodge started to leave.

"One more thing." Barnett smiled kindly. "Don't forget to give that present to Miss Martin. Otherwise, all that bother in Ellie Poston's store will have been for nothing."

"You're right about that." Caleb Hodge straightened his hat and left. He was eager to get to the play.

Alone, Dusty Barnett did a quick inspection of the rest of the room but found nothing of interest. That didn't surprise him. The shameful items Dog Bark had talked about had already been uncovered. As he began to turn off the lamp, the sheriff thought about how he would uncover the accomplice who had been aiding the phony Brett Connors.

"Maybe I should try some theatrics myself," he said in a stage whisper.

Chapter Sixteen

Phoebe Martin felt both excited and exhausted as she stood at the front of the church taking a bow with the rest of the cast. *The Phantom Killer* had been performed faultlessly, or at least with only a few small mistakes that the cast could easily cover.

Victor Lamont raised a hand to silence the audience. "The Lamont Theatrical Troupe is honored to have been a part of this historical occasion, the first play ever to be performed in Dawson, Arizona. But we could not have done it without the help of one of your own citizens. Let's express our appreciation for a very talented young lady, Phoebe Martin!"

The members of the troupe took a step back, leaving Phoebe standing alone to acknowledge the loud applause. For Phoebe Martin, the moment seemed incredibly magical. People who only a few days before had been gossiping about her were now on their feet applauding and waving. She turned to acknowledge the rest of the cast and saw that Charles Stafford and Bert Lassiter, two men she had regarded as creepy, were now smiling graciously and appearing to be true gentlemen.

The next hour was a whirlwind as the whole town gathered around the young woman, telling her what a wonderful job she had done. Nobody seemed to want to leave the church. Phoebe finally had to announce, truthfully, that she needed to change back into her own clothes and return two dresses to the Lamonts.

Walking toward the hotel with the costumes in her hand, Phoebe found herself waving at just about everyone she passed. People were not only friendly, they were, despite all the earlier comments about theater people, respectful.

As Phoebe stepped onto the second floor of the hotel, she saw Victor Lamont coming out of his room. "I was just going to check with Bert and Charles," he said. "We're pulling out early tomorrow. I want to thank you again for . . ."

Phoebe Martin felt oddly depressed. Victor was being cordial and polite, but it was obvious that his mind was on tomorrow morning. Understandable. But how could magic as powerful as she had experienced only an hour ago diminish so quickly?

". . . Jessica is putting away the costumes now. I know she wants to say good-bye to you." The head of the Lamont Theatrical Troupe went down the hall to confer with his two actors.

Phoebe walked into the Lamonts' room, where Jessica was carefully placing clothes in the large trunk that

Phoebe had last seen on the night Harold Benson was killed.

"You're right on time! Those two dresses are my last items to pack." Jessica Lamont looked as beautiful as ever, but there seemed to be a wistfulness about her. Phoebe wondered if the actress was experiencing the same sense of letdown that now afflicted her.

"We received a wire from Mamie Thompson today," Jessica said as she placed the dresses in the trunk. "She'll join us in Tombstone. I told you about Mamie, didn't I? She has played Connie Smith before—"

Jessica Lamont turned toward her companion, and a silent communication ran between the two women. Jessica abandoned the trunk and put her arms around Phoebe in a quick hug.

"You were terrific tonight!" Jessica stepped back and gave Phoebe a look of admiration and respect. She wasn't acting. "Your performance gave a special energy to our entire company. Tonight, the people of Dawson saw a play that matched anything running in New York or Philadelphia. You could be a first-rate actress, Phoebe. But don't do it."

"I don't understand."

"During this week, with everything you had to do, you still found time to visit the widow of that poor Mr. Benson who was murdered. You insisted that we stop a rehearsal and pray for that terrible man who shot at Charles to be caught before he could hurt others."

"Well, yes, but—"

"I could never do anything like that!" Jessica looked away and began to fuss with her hair. In the process, she might have brushed away some tears—Phoebe couldn't tell. But when the actress looked back, she was totally composed. "Things were not very nice for me when I was a child. The world was such a hard, ugly, terrible place, I decided to have no part of it. I created a fantasy world, and that is where I live."

"But you are such a good actress—"

"Thank you. But there is so little an actress can do. I come into a town, give a performance, and leave. People enjoy it, yes. But the next morning they wake up, and all their problems are still there. I can't help with those problems. You can, Phoebe. That's why you must stay in the real world."

"You do more for people than you think, Jessica. Remember what Robbie Gosden said at the town hall meeting? A play gives us something nice to think about on those days when nothing nice is happening."

A look of absolute bliss washed across Jessica's face. "I live for moments like that." That look diminished a bit. "But you can live for much more, Phoebe. Good luck out there in the real world. And, remember, you helped to give this town a fabulous evening the people will never forget."

Phoebe Martin stepped out of the hotel and paused on the boardwalk. Dawson was quiet except for the usual noise coming out of the saloons. She began to wonder about the town gossips who had rattled their tongues about her all week and then applauded her tonight. How would they treat her in church tomorrow morning?

"Evening, Phoebe."

Phoebe turned around to find a man who was fidgeting like a boy wearing new Sunday clothes for the first time. "Why, good evening, Caleb. I'm sorry, I didn't notice you standing by the door there. Guess my mind was a million miles away."

Caleb Hodge approached her slowly. He was carrying a decorative box that could only have come from Ellie Poston's store. "I couldn't get near you after the play. It seemed like the whole town had you surrounded. Afterward, I went to your place, and Amos told me that you had come here."

"Yes, I had to return my costumes."

"Phoebe, I know that you gave me permission to call you by your first name. But if you want to take it back, I wouldn't blame you."

"There's no need for that, Caleb. In fact, I would feel a lot safer if the deputy sheriff of Dawson would accompany me as I walk home."

"Be honored to." Caleb touched his hat with one hand and almost dropped the box in the process.

As they strolled together, the deputy sheriff began to tell Phoebe that Dusty Barnett was only a few steps away from arresting Harold Benson's killer. The lawman's voice turned to a mumble as he explained that he had to be quiet about the details, and then, suddenly,

Caleb began to blurt out a speech he'd been thinking about much of the day. "I need to apologize for all that hogwash I blabbered to you about playacting. Playacting is nothing like being a saloon girl, and I'm powerful sorry I said that."

"I accept your apology, Caleb, and I do understand. I mean, this is the first time Dawson has ever had a play. It's easy to get confused."

Caleb Hodge smiled and continued in an almost jubilant voice. "I got to thinking about things, and, after all, you stand up in front of a lot of people every week when you sing those solos in church. That's sort of what playacting is like, singing in church."

"Well, yes, that's an interesting thought," Phoebe said as the couple stopped in front of Martin's Restaurant. "I appreciate your walking me home like this."

"Happy to oblige. You did a fine job of playacting tonight."

"Thank you, Caleb."

"What's more, you're even prettier than Jessica Lamont!"

"Thank you, Caleb."

The deputy sheriff held up the box he had been carrying. "I got this for you as sort of a congratulations for doing such a good job in the play. It's nothing much, but I hope you like it."

Phoebe Martin employed her new acting skills to pretend that she was noticing the box for the first time. "Why, thank you, Caleb." She took the present, untied the ribbon, and carefully lifted the lid. "A hat! This is so nice of you."

"Ellie Poston said that this hat is what all the ladies are wearing in the east right now."

"Well, I'll be wearing mine in church tomorrow. It's so beautiful. Thank—"

"Speaking of church and all, would it be okay if I was to sit with you tomorrow—I mean, with you and your mother and father?"

"That would be wonderful. I'm sure they would both enjoy having you with us."

Caleb managed to shake his nervous demeanor and look directly into Phoebe's eyes. "I miss those breakfasts we used to have at the restaurant."

"So do I."

"Now that you're finished with the playacting and all, maybe we could start again on Monday, after I finish my first round."

"I'd like that, Caleb."

The nervousness returned, and Hodge began to look around him for no apparent reason. "Guess I should get back to the office. After all, I am on duty."

"You be careful, you and Mr. Barnett. This killer you were telling me about sounds like a dangerous man."

The deputy shrugged his shoulders and stepped off the boardwalk. "No need to fret."

"And, Caleb . . ."

Hodge paused and looked at her. "Yes?"

"Thank you again for the hat. It's beautiful."

"Real glad you like it." Caleb smiled broadly, touched his own hat with two fingers, and began to stride toward the sheriff's office.

Phoebe smiled as she examined the hat. There were far too many ribbons and artificial flowers. The hat was so fancy, it looked silly. Ellie Poston had probably been trying to sell the thing for months. A gleam must have come into her eye when she saw poor Caleb walk into her store.

Phoebe lifted the hat from the box for a closer look. She would work on it tonight and have it looking better by morning. The young woman laughed out loud. She was certain that Caleb would not notice the changes, but, of course, he would notice that she was wearing the hat he had bought her.

"I will wear it, that's for sure," Phoebe whispered to herself.

Phoebe began to think back on her conversation with Jessica Lamont. The actress had been right about a lot of things. The world could be a hard place—Phoebe knew that. She thought about Harold Benson, one of the nicest men she had ever known, lying in a pool of blood, the victim of a brutal murder. She remembered Clara's terrible scream upon seeing her husband's corpse. Phoebe had embraced the elderly woman and felt her terrible shaking.

A loud meow sounded from within the restaurant. Phoebe placed the hat back into the box, opened the door, and crouched down as Horatio slithered out onto the boardwalk. "So, what did you think of my performance tonight?"

The cat purred and rubbed its head against Phoebe's arm. Phoebe scratched behind his right ear. "I guess that means you liked it. But, according to Father, you slept on his lap the whole time."

Horatio meowed again. Phoebe began to pet him with long, slow strokes. "You're right. I need to stop playacting and stop fretting over all the bad things in the world. Reverend Colt would say that I should start counting my blessings."

The young woman placed her fancy box on the boardwalk and lifted Horatio into her arms as she stood up. "I do have a lot of blessings. There's Mother and Father, you . . ."

Phoebe caressed the cat's fur with her cheek, then slowly stepped off the boardwalk and made her way to the middle of the road. The light inside the sheriff's office shone brightly, and she could see Caleb Hodge standing outside the office talking with Reverend Colt. Caleb was facing away from her, but there was no mistaking that strong, well-muscled back.

Phoebe turned to Horatio, whose head rested against her shoulder. "Jessica is right. The world is a hard place, but there is a lot that is good and decent in it. We all have been given blessings, me more than most." She looked back up the road to where Caleb was now entering the sheriff's office.

"I have been very blessed," she said.

Chapter Seventeen

The performance of The Phantom Killer *was a fabulous success. The denizens of Dawson, Arizona, were uplifted in that special way that only art can uplift. People left the small church more enlightened about the tremendous beauties that life can offer but at the same time fearful. This town still lives in terror that some madman, driven by hidden motives and impulses no one understands, may once again put on the dark and demonic costume of the crazed killer in the play they saw performed tonight and, in a quick, bloody act of murder, claim another innocent life.*

Bradley Stevens reread the last paragraph in his story. "Good, very good," he told himself approvingly. Of course, his editor back in Philadelphia would be irritated by that last sentence, claiming it was too long and run on.

"Complain all you want. You'll print the story exactly the way I wrote it and be happy you have it." Stevens sneered in the direction of the editor, whom he envisioned standing in front of him. "I know you and everyone else in the office were laughing at me. 'Send Bradley Stevens, that insufferable snob, out west. Let him try ordering one of those fancy wines at a café in Dawson, Arizona!' Well, who's laughing now? My articles about the phantom killer are being printed in papers throughout the country. Maybe even in Europe! Bradley Stevens is the most valuable reporter you've got!"

The editor vanished, and Stevens looked around his hotel room. He knew that his standing at the *Tribune* had greatly improved, and he knew that it wouldn't last. Within a few months people would be complaining again that his copy was too wordy and snobbish.

The reporter began to work on the letter of resignation that would accompany his story to Philadelphia. He provided the *Tribune* with an address where the paper could send his final check, then felt a sense of glee as he wrote:

Having witnessed Dawson's first play, I will now start the first newspaper in this fair town. No doubt, I will meet many heroic individuals and encounter thrilling adventures. I will make the accounts of my life in the west available to newspapers in the east. Of course, out of respect for our past association, I will give the Tribune *the first bid on my exciting accounts of life in the Arizona Territory.*

Bradley Stevens laughed as he slapped his left hand onto the desk. "I am going to become a very rich man, and the money from the *Tribune* will only be a small part of it."

Two short knocks sounded on the hotel room door. The reporter felt embarrassed, wondering if anyone had overheard him talking to himself.

"Who's there, please?" There was no response. As Stevens approached the door, he saw that an envelope had been slipped under it. He hastily picked up the white object and opened the door to see a vacant first-floor hallway.

His room was close to the lobby, but as he scampered out, he saw that no one was there. The desk clerk had retired for the night. A pleasant aroma began to fill the reporter's nostrils. The envelope was heavily perfumed.

Bradley Stevens almost ran back to his room. He wanted to read this letter in private. The reporter ripped open the envelope and had his strongest hopes confirmed. The page was covered with a clumsy scrawl, but what could you expect from a girl who was brought up in such a primitive part of the country? Phoebe Martin had probably never seen the inside of a schoolroom. No doubt, that was part of why she was so attracted to him. He represented the culture and sophistication that had been totally absent from her life.

Stevens pulled out his pocket watch. There was still a half hour till midnight, the time Phoebe wanted to meet him outside of town. According to the letter, she would have a carriage ready. Where would she take him?

"Who knows?" Stevens said aloud, no longer embarrassed to be talking to himself. "Maybe there's an abandoned ranch house somewhere nearby." The reporter walked to the desk and briefly skimmed his article. He had written some very nice things about Phoebe Martin's performance that evening. *I'll quote those kind comments to her tonight,* he thought.

He went to the mirror and carefully arranged his hair to cover the fact that he was balding. His efforts were for naught, as they always were in this particular endeavor, but Bradley Stevens was too excited to care.

Before leaving the room, he tore up the letter into small pieces as Phoebe had requested. The poor girl was afraid that their rendezvous would be discovered. Well, he couldn't blame her. Dawson was a small town, and caution was required. After all, he wanted to have many other secret rendezvous with Miss Phoebe Martin.

Bradley Stevens left the hotel and, following the instructions in the letter, began a brisk walk to the south end of town. Once he was past the stores and houses, the darkness began to spook him, and his steps became more cautious. This was not Philadelphia, where myriad lights battled the night; only the distant stars and moon provided a modicum of help.

A horse whinnied from nearby. The reporter forgot his anxieties and began to follow the sound. He came upon a black carriage attached to a large bay. Stevens quickly advanced toward the carriage, then stopped when he got to the horse. He forced a smile and patted the head of the nag, trying to look casual. Phoebe Martin couldn't be allowed to know that he was afraid of horses.

He stepped away from the animal and began to look around. "Miss Martin?"

An explosion of red drenched the darkness of night.

Chapter Eighteen

Bradley Stevens awoke to a nightmare. His head throbbed with pain. His rib cage was being steadily assaulted. He tried to cry out for help, but his mouth was gagged.

Panic engulfed the reporter as he realized that his hands and feet were tied and his entire body was strewn over a horse. A slight lift of his head revealed surrounding rocks. Stevens' panic intensified. The mountains had looked so majestic from afar, but here they seemed desolate and foreboding.

The horse stopped, and the reporter could hear someone ahead of him dismounting. Stevens was lifted off the horse, carried a short distance, then dropped to the ground in a very ungentle manner. Pain and nausea engulfed the reporter, and he yearned for the luxury of unconsciousness. But, somehow, he sensed that the mercy of blacking out was not to be granted him.

Stevens could hear approaching footsteps and whistling. The whistling was cheerful but did nothing to lift the reporter's spirits. The man that most of Dawson called Brett Connors came into view. He placed an object down carefully beside a boulder, then tossed a collection of branches onto the ground.

"You know, I haven't learned all the skills of being a westerner yet." The imposter spoke in a voice that was robust and friendly. "I had to bring some stuff from Dawson just to build a campfire. Why, I know fellas who can come up here to the mountains and build a fire with just a couple of twigs and some mesquite. How do you suppose they do that?"

The actor threw up his hands in an exaggerated gesture. "Would you look at me? Asking questions of a man who's tied up and gagged. My mama always said that it was impossible to teach me manners. Guess she was right."

The bogus Brett Connors cheerfully ambled over to Stevens, removed his gag, pulled out a pocketknife, and cut the ropes. Blood once again flowed into the reporter's hands and feet.

The big man looked down at his prisoner. "I apologize for being so rude."

Stevens' voice was little more than a hoarse whisper. "You wrote the note, not Phoebe Martin. That was your carriage—"

"Right!" The smile remained. "The one I told you about, with the dent in the right wheel that would make it easy to track and identify. That's why we had to steal the buckboard."

Bradley Stevens realized that his captor's outward friendliness was a sham, but he still wanted to encourage it. "What is your real name anyway?"

A wild anger flared in the big man's eyes, but his demeanor remained outwardly friendly. "Why, Bradley, I think you should call me by the name I used on the stage. Stuart Hahn. Remember all the fun you had with that name? Remember that brilliant line of yours that they used in the headline of the review?"

"Listen, that was—"

The bogus Brett Connors lifted his arms and slowly moved them in opposite directions as if reading words written in the stars. "The day after the most important performance of my life, where I played the lead role in *Hamlet* at the Franklin Theater in Philadelphia, the headline on the review in the *Tribune* read, 'Stuart Hahn's *Hamlet* is a Ham Stew.'"

"Nothing personal, Stuart—"

Stuart Hahn gave a loud, hard laugh. "No need to say you're sorry, Bradley. The line was brilliant. You had the whole city of Philadelphia laughing at me."

Hahn walked over to the pile of sticks he had tossed to the ground and began to arrange them carefully for a fire. "Guess I should thank you. I got booted from the theatrical company in Philadelphia and joined a traveling troupe that did light comedies. That's how I met Brett Connors in Denver. I killed him and took on the greatest role of my career. How do you think I'm doing?"

"I can help you, Stuart. I'll—"

Hahn stopped his work and looked directly at Stevens. The broad smile was still on his lips and the hatred still in his eyes. "You know, when I first got that wire from Philadelphia that Bradley Stevens was coming to Dawson, I hoped that you wouldn't recognize me. After all, I was in costume that night you saw me in *Hamlet*, and—"

"I didn't recognize you at first—"

Stuart Hahn took a few steps toward his prisoner, pointing a finger at him. "Then came that afternoon when you told me that you knew who I was and had figured out what I was up to." Hahn stopped pointing and started laughing. "You made me mad, Bradley. I'll admit it. You wanted in on the scheme. In other words, you wanted in on the money. Then I saw you again that evening at the sheriff's office, and you started blabbering about staying in town and starting a newspaper."

Stuart Hahn forgot about building a fire and began to walk toward his prisoner. "But that night, I realized that you were a man I could work with. You broke into my house and stole the phantom killer costume and two guns. You appeared on the roof of Behan's Gun Shop, firing in my direction. Warning shots, I guess you could call them."

"I didn't shoot to hit you or anyone else." The words tumbled from the reporter's mouth. Stuart Hahn was now, once again, standing directly over him.

"A good actor must be flexible, able to handle anything that might happen onstage." Hahn gave the reporter a hard kick in the ribs. Stevens' body convulsed as he released a high-pitched whine. "I improvised very well that night," the actor continued in a mock friendly voice. "I shot Jeb Gavens and made it look like an accident. Of course, that set off a big ruckus, leaving plenty of time for you to get off that roof and get out of sight. Otherwise you would have been in jail crying your heart out to the sheriff. I gave a good performance that night, Bradley. Too bad you couldn't write up one of your clever reviews."

Stevens tried to speak, but all that came out was a squeak. He fell silent, trying to think of a way he could regain the actor's trust. After all, the night Hahn had shot Gavens, he had talked with Stuart and convinced him that they could become partners. He had helped the actor steal the buckboard and horses and rob the stage in order to get the mailbag. Now his life depended on reestablishing that partnership.

Hahn suddenly turned his head leftward. "Did you hear something?" His voice was serious, the smile gone.

"No, nothing."

"Guess this cold night is affecting my mind." The false cheeriness returned. "I need to get that fire going." Stuart Hahn returned to the collection of branches, then pulled a box of matches from his pocket and lit one. He crouched down and tried to apply the flame to the wood. The light flickered and vanished.

"See what I told you?" Hahn shook his head and grinned. "Good thing that Brett Connors was an easterner like me. Otherwise I would have failed at the part, just like I did with the famous prince. You would have given me another bad review."

Bradley Stevens realized that he was just as helpless as he had been when he was tied up. An intense pain ravaged his head, and he knew that several of his ribs were broken. The reporter wasn't sure that he could stand up, never mind run.

Besides, where would he run to? The mountains were a horrifying place to him, filled with treacherous beasts of the wild. His only hope was to talk his way out of it. "My days of writing reviews are over, Stuart. I'm going to be a small-town newspaperman. I can help you—"

"There!" Flames crackled over the collection of branches. Stuart Hahn stood up and admired his handiwork. "I'm not a greedy man, Bradley. Cutting you into the act would have made for a three-way split, since I'm bringing in a friend from Philadelphia who specializes in keeping crooked books. But there are going to be some stage robberies over the next few years. A lot of money is going to vanish. Having a newspaperman to help folks accept my version of the events would have been helpful. Then you had to go and betray me, Bradley."

"I don't know what you're talking about!"

Hatred momentarily consumed all of Stuart Hahn's face. He walked in a straight, fast manner toward his prisoner. Stevens folded himself into a fetal position, covering his head. "Please! Don't kick me again!"

"When I got home tonight, I found a red bandanna,

with holes cut into it for the eyes, pinned to my bedroom door with a knife." Hahn yelled angrily at his prisoner. "I checked under the mattress. Nothing there but another red bandanna. I'm getting a little tired of you breaking into my house, Bradley!"

"I didn't—"

"Where's the picture?" The actor's voice became even louder and more intense.

"Picture?"

"The Connors family portrait—the one we stole from the stagecoach. What did you do with it, Bradley?"

"I haven't seen that picture since the holdup. Honest, I'm telling the truth!"

Hahn smirked at his prisoner, then turned and walked back toward the fire. "I'm almost glad to hear you say that. You see, I've learned some very important things about myself lately."

The actor picked up the object he had tossed to the ground before building the fire. Bradley Stevens couldn't tell what it was, but his sense of terror increased, and his body began to tremble.

"I'm a good actor!" Hahn pointed the long, stick-shaped object at his prisoner. "A whole town believes that I am a responsible, good-hearted man named Brett Connors. I don't need your opinion, Mr. Bradley Stevens!"

The reporter wanted desperately to say something in his defense, but his mind was scrambled. He muttered a stream of babble as saliva coursed down his chin.

"The second thing I discovered is that I really do enjoy killing. Murdering Brett Connors was fun. Same with Harold Benson. I strangled old Harold first, put on my phantom killer costume, then waited to hear his dear wife coming. Clara always brought Harold dinner when he worked late. I put two bullets into the old cuss and then ran outside as the phantom killer. I needed a witness that the phantom had killed poor Harold. Luck was with me that night. I ended up with two witnesses."

The actor took a few steps toward the fire and thrust the end of the object into the flames. Bradley Stevens let out a another high-pitched whine. "That's what they call a branding iron!"

Stuart Hahn laughed and nodded. "Never used one of these things before. You'll have to show me a bit of patience. I could be a mite clumsy at first."

"Please . . ."

"Where's the picture, Bradley?" Hahn pulled the branding iron from the fire, examined the end, and then returned it to the blaze. "You see, I have a sense that my luck is starting to run low. It wouldn't be a good idea for me to risk getting caught searching the hotel room of a man who is missing. That would create suspicion, and, of course, you could have hidden the thing someplace else. No, Bradley, you're going to tell me exactly where that picture is."

"You're going to kill me." Stevens began to cry loudly. "Whatever I say, I'm going to die on this wretched mountain."

"Maybe, maybe not." Hahn once again pulled the

branding iron from the blaze and examined it. This time he appeared satisfied.

"Tell me where the picture is, Bradley, and—who knows?—I just might let you live."

Stuart Hahn walked slowly but purposefully toward his prisoner, pointing the hot end of the iron directly at him. Bradley Stevens let out a scream that was suddenly punctuated by the sound of a Winchester firing into the air.

"Throw down that branding iron, Connors or Hahn, whatever your name is!"

The actor looked up at a familiar figure, who was now standing beside a boulder. "Why, sure, Dusty. You know that I have always been a man who helps maintain law and order."

The actor casually tossed the implement to one side. The iron clinked against a couple of rocks as Barnett moved hurriedly downward, stopping beside Bradley Stevens. "Since you're being so cooperative, Hahn, why don't you slowly unfasten your gun belt and let it drop to the ground?"

Stuart Hahn laughed and shrugged his shoulders. "You pulled one over on me, didn't you, Sheriff? You stole the picture and made it look like poor Bradley took it."

"That's right. I had pegged you as Harold's killer. But, of course, it couldn't have been you in the costume last night on top of Behan's Gun Shop. I figured Stevens for that job, but I needed to find out just how deep the reporter was in. I've been following him. Now, take off that gun belt."

Hahn smiled broadly and shook his head. "Pardon me for being rude, Dusty. You know my mama said—"

"I know what she said. I've been listening in for a while. Take off the gun belt."

Stuart Hahn began to undo the buckle of the belt that held the holster for his .44. "How did you figure Bradley for the other phantom?"

"I kept thinking on why a buckboard was needed for a stagecoach holdup. There was no reason, unless the man in the phantom outfit couldn't ride a horse. After that, Mr. Stevens just naturally came to mind. I talked to the town's merchants. Stevens never met with them to discuss starting a paper. All that big talk in my office was aimed at Brett Connors, or the man I thought was Brett Connors. Bradley fired at you from the roof of the gun shop as a way of pressuring you to let him in on the deception. To let you know that he had the guts to be a fellow crook and the guts to expose you."

Hahn dropped his gun belt. "Dusty, you're wasting your talents as a small-town sheriff. I bet the Pinkertons will offer you a job when news gets out that you captured two phantoms." Hahn smirked and pointed to himself. "One will hang. The other will go to jail."

Something hard crashed against Barnett's ankles. Dusty cursed himself for ignoring Bradley Stevens. As the lawman hit the ground, Stevens grabbed the Winchester and tried to yank it from the sheriff's hands.

Barnett pushed the reporter away as the sound of hurried footsteps echoed in the mountains.

"Hahn, you fool, don't run!" Stevens' shout was a desperate plea. "Together we can escape, stay out of jail!"

Hahn ignored the reporter and kept running up a mountain trail. Barnett took off after him, noting that the actor had picked up his gun. Stuart Hahn was a fast runner, but Barnett hoped that the actor's unfamiliarity with mountain terrain would slow him a bit.

The lawman briefly smiled as he ran. That old saw about the stars and moon being brighter in the mountains did seem to be true. He had no trouble keeping his prey in sight.

Hahn suddenly stopped and looked down. Then the actor bolted behind a boulder on his left side. There was nowhere nearby for Barnett to take cover. The sheriff realized that he was also the prey as he dropped to the ground. A shot scattered some small stones nearby.

The lawman knew that he had to get the most out of his first shot with the Winchester. "Not bad shooting for an actor from Philadelphia, Hahn!"

The actor couldn't resist the opportunity for a bow. His head and shoulders rose above the boulder. "Thanks, Dusty! I've been practicing since—"

Barnett's shot hit the boulder only a few inches from its target. Hahn gave a yell of shock and fear as some chips exploded off the large rock and scraped his face. The actor fired again at the sheriff, but this time the bullet flew harmlessly until it became a distant echo. The second shot from the Winchester came perilously close to Hahn and caused him to lose his balance and fall.

Hahn scrambled back onto his feet and peered over the boulder. Barnett had moved. Was that him behind that large, scraggly bush? He wasn't sure, but he knew the sheriff was advancing on him. He thought about running up the mountain by some other route than the trail but doubted if he had the necessary mountain knowledge or skills. Holding on to his gun, he bent down low and resumed his desperate run up the trail.

Barnett muttered under his breath as he dashed from behind the bush. The mountains were filled with predators. He could only hope that two-legged creatures would pose the only danger on this night.

Stuart Hahn gained speed and put a little more distance between himself and his pursuer. But he knew that wasn't enough. Barnett would keep after him, and the sheriff knew the mountain terrain and was a better shot.

The actor spotted his escape. A large cave stood only a few yards up the mountain from him. Stuart Hahn turned and fired two reckless shots. Barnett jumped sideways for cover. Hahn ran with full fury into the cave, hoping the lawman hadn't seen his detour.

Hahn was stunned and frightened by the total darkness that surrounded him. He had never before been in a place totally devoid of light. But the actor's fear turned into a frantic hope. Even if Barnett had seen him enter the cave, the sheriff's prowess with a gun wouldn't mean much in this sightless hole. Bent over only slightly, the killer edged forward into the constant night.

Dusty Barnett arrived at the mouth of the cave and leaned against the hard rock to think over his next move. The planning had to be brief. He knew his prey was in the cover of darkness and stood a chance of getting away. Barnett took a long, deep breath and, still holding on to the Winchester, entered the cave.

Inside, the sheriff could hear the distant sound of dripping water but nothing else. He ran in place for a moment. The trick worked. Hurried footsteps sounded from ahead.

A low, visceral growl rumbled in the darkness, then exploded into a terrifying screech. The sound of scrambling feet was followed by a loud, painful cry from Stuart Hahn as he fell in a hopeless attempt to defend himself. "Help, Barnett—wolf!"

Through the horrifying noise of the actor's wails and the beast's merciless attack, Dusty could hear the yapping of small pups. The lawman fired his Winchester toward the side of the cave. The shot ricocheted, creating a loud, threatening echo. A roar came from the she wolf, who retreated several steps, shielding her litter of pups. Stuart Hahn remained on the ground, his body twisting as he let out sharp cries of pain. "Lost my gun . . ." His voice was filled with panic. The wolf resumed her low growl.

Barnett spoke in a soft, low monotone. "Hahn, stop

blubbering. Listen carefully." The sheriff took a few cautious steps in the direction of the growl as Stuart Hahn became still. "A hunter once told me that a quiet voice can calm a wolf—sometimes. A cry might cause her to attack."

Barnett could now see the wolf's eyes. The two orbs looked suspended in air, as if the darkness of the cave was itself a living creature. Barnett thought about attempting a shot but decided that it would be too risky. Instead, he continued to speak in a low voice. "Her mate is probably hunting. I'd sure like to get out of here before he gets back."

Dusty Barnett wanted to turn and leave a killer to the horrible death he deserved. As the sheriff moved steadily toward those threatening eyes, he instinctively touched his badge with one hand. If that badge meant anything at all, he knew that he had to at least try to save Stuart Hahn. The lawman could only hope that he and the actor didn't become a family dinner.

The wolf's growl intensified. Barnett gripped his Winchester a bit harder but continued to speak in that soft, low monotone. "Hahn, I can't see you. Make as little noise as you can—just enough to let me know where you are."

The actor whined something. Two demonic eyes floated forward a few inches, then halted. "Okay, Hahn, hold out an arm, and don't make a sound when you do it."

Barnett's left hand grasped air twice and then connected with Stuart Hahn. As the sheriff pulled Hahn backward, he hoped the she wolf would recognize the dragging sounds as sounds of retreat. As the cave's mouth came into view, Barnett increased his speed. Outside the cave, he let out a loud sigh, set his Winchester beside the dark cavity, and crouched over his prisoner.

"Think you can make it back to the horses?" Barnett still spoke in his calm, monotone voice. "I can clean and bandage the wound a lot better there."

Stuart Hahn babbled something and seemed to nod his head. The man was swimming in pain and delirium, but Dusty thought Hahn could understand what was being said to him.

"Yes, Sheriff! By all means, let's get back to the horses. I've just been there, and look at what I found."

Barnett slowly lifted himself up and faced Bradley Stevens. Stevens was crouched over and barely able to maintain his balance, but his hands gripped the Henry he had taken from Hahn's saddle and now pointed at Barnett.

"Stevens, you're not only a snake, you're a stupid snake."

"Look, Sheriff, I can make you a hero! Promise me that when we get to town, you'll tell people that I helped you capture the phantom killer. I'll have your name all over the front page of—"

Barnett pointed at the Henry. "The next time you point a gun at somebody, make sure it's loaded."

Bradley Stevens looked down at the object in his hands. Dusty snatched it away from him.

"That's an old trick." Dusty Barnett looked contemptuously at the reporter. "If I were you, I wouldn't tell the folks back in Philadelphia that you fell for it."

Stevens lurched toward the rifle but fell to the hard ground, where he began to cry.

"Might as well cry for yourself, because no one is going to cry for you," Barnett declared angrily. "You have a talent for words. A talent you could have used for fine things. But you wasted it on a lot of selfish foolishness. Nobody is going to cry for you, Stevens."

Bradley Stevens continued to cry as Stuart Hahn moaned in pain only a few feet away. Barnett groaned in disgust. "Guess I got two sorry specimens of mankind to get back to town."

Chapter Nineteen

The next week was a festive one for Dawson as reporters from the east arrived to cover what they labeled The Phantom Killer Trials. Some locals complained about the outsiders, but the town's hotel was full, and business was brisk at the saloons and restaurants.

The circuit judge announced that first he would try the case of Bradley Stevens, and then he'd take on Stuart Hahn. But before all that, he was taking a day off to nurse a bad cold.

While the judge rested, the reporters devoted their time to interviewing Phoebe Martin, who told the press that, no, she didn't think watching a performance of *The Phantom Killer* or similar melodramas had turned Stuart Hahn and Bradley Stevens into cold-blooded outlaws. A photographer from New York took a picture of Phoebe, which became part of an exhibit, *Portraits of the West,* that toured throughout the northeast. A small sign posted beside Phoebe's portrait identified her as: *Phoebe Martin, a young woman raised in the Arizona*

176

Territory. When an actress in a touring theatrical company unexpectedly resigned her position, Miss Martin stepped in and took a lead role in the first play ever performed in Dawson, Arizona.

On the night before the trials began, Reverend Colt and Dusty Barnett had dinner together at Martin's Restaurant. After their food arrived, Colt gathered some green beans together on a fork and commented. "I'm hoping that my successor will not have to do too many trials, either as the prosecutor or defense attorney."

Barnett cut his beef. "Understandable. A preacher has plenty to do without—"

"It's not that," the clergyman said as he put down his fork. "Dawson needs to move away from the miners' court way of doing justice. We need—"

"Excuse me, gentlemen." The newcomer was a handsome, well-dressed man with a scholarly appearance. He addressed the town's only clergyman. "I believe you are Reverend Colt. I mean—"

Paul Colten had been in situations like this many times before. Instinctively he moved to make the newcomer feel comfortable. He smiled, stood up, and extended his hand. "Reverend Colt is just fine. Everyone calls me that."

"Sherm Cummings." There were handshakes all around; then the newcomer got to the point. "I'm a reporter for the *Philadelphia Tribune*. My editor has asked me to apologize to you on behalf of the paper. Mr. Bradley Stevens was not well liked at the *Tribune,* and, well, I'm afraid that sending him out here was a bit of a joke. As it turns out, the joke was not very funny. We are sorry."

Both men assured Sherm Cummings that there was no need for an apology and invited the reporter to join them for dinner. As they talked, Barnett noted that the newcomer seemed quite taken with the west. *Maybe Dawson will soon get a newspaper after all,* he mused.

When Barnett returned to his office, he found both Caleb Hodge and Phoebe Martin waiting for him. The young man and woman were both laughing, though neither was telling jokes. The sheriff immediately understood what this was all about and suddenly felt a bit giddy himself.

"Caleb and I have some news for you, Sheriff."

"Now, just what might that be?" Barnett closed the office door behind him and placed his hat on the rack.

"You are the first to know, outside of our families." Phoebe beamed. "We're getting married!"

Barnett feigned surprise, or tried to, then found himself hugging Phoebe Martin. He didn't know exactly how that had happened, and when he let go of her, he felt a bit embarrassed. "I've got some news of my own. You two won't be starting life together on a deputy's salary. Not for long, anyway."

The lawman explained how he had purchased the gun shop from Leonard Behan and would be taking it over soon. "But don't think you're getting rid of me, Sheriff

Hodge. I'll be right across the street, in case you need an extra deputy. In fact, you're going to have trouble keeping me out of any trouble that comes up. Fixing guns all day can be pretty dull work."

There was nervous laughter. Both Phoebe and Caleb seemed pleased with Dusty's news but uncertain how to respond. Phoebe finally said in a soft voice, "I need to get back to the restaurant. Don't want to get my father into one of his grumpy moods."

Barnett accompanied Caleb and Phoebe to the front door, where Phoebe suddenly whirled around, gave the sheriff a kiss on the cheek, and whispered in his ear, "I'm so happy Caleb has you to help him."

The sheriff stood at the window and watched the couple walk off, holding hands and laughing together. He didn't understand why, but he knew that Phoebe's whispered words were very important to him. He'd remember them for the rest of his life and do everything he could to help Caleb.

Barnett felt a bit of moisture gathering in one eye and hastily brushed it away. "Turning into a sentimental fool in my old age," he said to an empty office.

Bradley Stevens was defended by a lawyer provided by his former employer. The defense presented a strong, rational case; Stevens was not directly involved in the murder of Harold Benson. He became an accomplice only after the fact. He deserved punishment but not the noose. Reverend Colt's case for the prosecution was a simple laying-out of the facts. He agreed with the defense that Stevens should not be hanged.

The trial took about two hours. After less than one hour of deliberation, a jury returned, and an ashen-faced Bradley Stevens was told that he would spend the next fifteen years of his life in prison. The former reporter was bent over, his entire body quivering as he left the courtroom. But Dusty Barnett had been right. No one wept for Bradley Stevens. He was a man who had been given much in life and had willfully squandered it all.

The next day the courtroom was packed, as people had been lining up early to attend the main event, the trial of Stuart Hahn, the man Dawson had known as Brett Connors. Clara Benson was present in the courtroom, flanked by Owen Connors and his wife. Owen was a distant cousin of the real Brett Connors, and the young couple was there to represent the family, as Abigail Connors' health was too frail for her to make the trip from Philadelphia.

The trial's beginning was dramatic, as Stuart Hahn announced that, "Your Honor, I will defend myself and prove that I am not an evil person, despite what might be said by some preacher who has a gun strapped to his waist when he pounds his pulpit."

Reverend Colt retorted with, "Your Honor, I may be a man who carries a gun, but I have only used it in self-defense. Stuart Hahn is a murderer with the blood of two men on his hands, and that is a fact that the prosecution will prove beyond a doubt in this courtroom."

In fact, the prosecution had to prove very little. Stuart Hahn formally pleaded innocent but then confessed to the charges against him during his opening statement to the jury. "Brett Connors was the spoiled son of a wealthy family. Harold Benson was old and weak. Neither man had much to look forward to here on earth. So I arranged for them to make the trip to heaven a bit early."

The jury didn't laugh. But they nodded their heads in agreement when Reverend Colt said, "The decision as to when a person leaves this earth is one that belongs in the realm of the Almighty. And I can assure you that the Lord is capable of handling this task without any assistance from Mr. Hahn."

The trial became a bizarre spectacle as Stuart Hahn tried repeatedly to elicit laughs from the courtroom. "I may be a cold-blooded killer, but, by golly, I'm a cold-blooded killer with a sense of humor." Hahn's demeanor became increasingly frantic as his jokes failed to engender even a few smiles.

Paul Colten ended his final summation to the jury in a quiet but determined voice. "All of you people know me. You know that in the past I have prosecuted killers and asked that they be spared the rope. But Stuart Hahn has not displayed even a touch of remorse for killing two people. In fact, he has made cruel jokes about his victims, knowing that Harold Benson's widow and two members of Brett Connors' family are in this courtroom. The Book of Ecclesiastes tells us that there is a time for everything, including a time to die. For Stuart Hahn, that time to die is now."

The jury agreed.

The verdict extended Dawson's festive mood for another few days as folks eagerly awaited the hanging. Children and adults alike watched as Dawson's first gallows was constructed directly in front of the sheriff's office. At the suggestion of Fred Bostick, wheels were placed under the gallows. This practical move made for a portable contraption that could be moved to the back of the sheriff's office when not in use and save the town the time and expense of constructing a new gallows every time a killer was sentenced to hang.

Many of the townspeople were impressed by Fred's cleverness, but others argued that the whole notion of building any kind of gallows was an unnecessary waste. After all, nature had provided a sturdy cottonwood just outside Dawson, which had served just fine as an instrument of execution. Why try to improve upon nature? The debate raged well into the night at the town's saloons.

Stuart Hahn's hanging was to take place at 1:00 P.M. on a Friday afternoon. On the morning of the execution, Reverend Colt spent an hour with the prisoner in his cell. As the pastor entered Dusty Barnett's office from the cell area, there was a look of confusion on his face.

"Did Hahn express any regret for—"

"No regret for killing two people," Colt hurriedly replied. "But he's despondent over the fact that his courtroom performance was such a failure. He's also very nervous."

Barnett gave a quick, sarcastic laugh. "Nothing unusual about that, after all."

Paul Colten waved his right hand back and forth as if erasing something from a blackboard. "No, that's not it. Hahn is nervous in a different way. He sort of reminds me of Phoebe Martin when I talked to her a few hours before the play. The young lady was nervous, of course, but still determined to do a good job with playing her part, and, well, she was looking forward to it. Stuart Hahn is the same way."

"You mean, he's looking forward to it?" Suddenly Barnett began to feel a bit nervous himself.

The sheriff's office held four grim-faced men: Dusty Barnett, Paul Colten, Caleb Hodge, and Stuart Hahn. Hahn's hands were tied behind his back. The clergyman pulled a watch from his frock coat. "One o'clock."

Barnett looked at the prisoner. "Let's go."

"Wait a minute!" Hahn's face looked incredulous. "We can't just walk out there willy-nilly."

The sheriff was a bit startled. "What—"

"Sheriff Barnett, you walk out the door first." Hahn's voice was slow and direct. He reminded Dusty of the way Victor Lamont had been speaking on the day the lawman walked in on a rehearsal of *The Phantom Killer.*

Stuart Hahn continued. "Reverend Colt, you follow the sheriff." Hahn nodded at the Bible in the pastor's right hand. "Could you read that part about 'The Lord is my shepherd'?"

"Psalm Twenty-Three."

"Yes. And read loudly," the condemned man instructed. "People should be able to hear your voice above the sound of our steps going up the gallows." Hahn turned to the one man still left without a part. "Deputy, you should follow me. That makes sense. You are there in case I try to escape."

"Anything to help fulfill the wishes of a dying man," Caleb Hodge replied.

Dusty Barnett's face held a look of astonishment over what he was witnessing. "Well, now that we all know how to do this proper like, maybe we should get started."

As the procession moved out of the sheriff's office toward the gallows that stood in the middle of the street, Barnett had to admit to himself that Hahn's ideas seemed to be effective. The large crowd fell completely silent, their eyes fixed on the four men as they stepped off the boardwalk and then paraded up the newly constructed stairs to where a strong rope, never used before, awaited them.

Stuart Hahn positioned himself under the noose, which now hung only a few feet over his head. His eyes darted to both sides to check the positions of his fellow players; Paul Colten and Caleb Hodge stood on his left, Dusty Barnett on his right. Hahn caught the eye of Caleb Hodge and nodded for him to take a few steps backward, so that he would be standing near the rear of the platform behind the clergyman. Though he felt odd doing so, Hodge followed the stage directions.

For a moment the actor looked down at the trapdoor he was standing on. He smiled and whispered, "Center stage" to the clergyman.

Reverend Colt was surprised by the remark but composed himself quickly and began the proceeding with a simple statement that Stuart Hahn had been found guilty of the murders of Harold Benson and Brett Connors and sentenced to hang. That sentence was now to be carried out. The clergyman concluded by looking at the prisoner. "Mr. Hahn, do you have anything to say?"

"Yes, Reverend, I do." Hahn's gaze ran over the crowd as he spoke. "I have committed horrible acts, for which I expect no mercy in this life or the next. I know that what I say now will mean nothing to them, but I apologize to the families of Harold Benson and Brett Connors. I also apologize to the citizens of this town for making a mockery of the courtroom."

Hahn paused briefly, gauging the effect of his words. Apparently satisfied, he continued, "But I do ask a favor of the people of Dawson. When you recall my heinous crimes, also remember how much I enjoyed being Brett Connors, a responsible, good man who always tried to do what was right. For all of my wretched crimes and deeds, there has always been a small something inside me that truly wanted to be that man." He turned to face the sheriff. "I am ready now for my punishment."

As Dusty Barnett place a canvas bag over the head of

the prisoner, he was stunned by the joy that glowed from Stuart Hahn's face. He was even more startled by the reaction from the mass of people surrounding the gallows. The response that had made the actor so happy.

They were applauding.

DATE DUE

6/1/12			
AUG 1 8 2012			
JUN 0 6 2012			
MAY 2 6 2014			
10/8/16			
NOV 3 0 2017			
JAN 0 4 2018			